Tales of Betsy-May

Tales of Betsy-May

Enid Blyton

Illustrated by
J. Gale Thomas

Dragon

Granada Publishing Limited
Published in 1970 by Dragon Books
Frogmore, St Albans, Herts AL2 2NF
Reprinted 1971, 1974

First published by Methuen & Co Ltd 1940
Copyright © Enid Blyton 1940
Made and printed in Great Britain by
C. Nicholls & Company Ltd
The Philips Park Press, Manchester
Set in Monotype Times

Contents

BETSY-MAY GOES TO THE POST

Betsy-May was a little girl. She wasn't very big, but she felt important. For the very first time she was going to post a letter by herself!

"It's only just down the road," Mother said. "Keep on the pavement, Betsy-May, and you'll be quite all right."

"Go straight there and back," said Nanny. "You are certainly a very big girl today!"

Betsy-May took the letter that Mother gave her, and went down the path to the gate. "Good-bye!" she said, and waved her hand. Then she stepped on to the pavement, and went down the road all by herself.

She met the milkman and he stared at her. "Good afternoon," said Betsy-May. "I'm going to post a letter all by myself."

"I thought you looked extra big to-day," said the milkman, and he went off, rattling his bottles.

Then Betsy-May met the newspaper boy and he looked at her. "Hallo!" he said.

"Hallo!" said Betsy-May. "I'm going to the post all by myself."

"Don't get lost, then!" said the newspaper boy and he went along whistling.

Betsy-May knew she wouldn't get lost. She could see the red pillar-box from where she stood. She walked along, feeling bigger and bigger.

She met old Mrs. Jack, and she smiled at her. Mrs. Jack smiled back.

"Where's your Mother?" she said. "Does she know you are out in the road?"

"Of course!" said Betsy-May, in a very grown-up voice. "She sent me to the post with this letter."

"Good gracious!" said Mrs. Jack. "Fancy you being big enough for that!"

Betsy-May laughed and went on. It was fun going out by herself and meeting people. Who would she see next?

It was the greengrocer coming along now, jerking the reins of his horse and singing a little song. He saw Betsy-May and waved.

"Good afternoon!" he said. "I hope you liked the oranges your Mother bought from me yesterday!"

"Yes, thank you," said Betsy-May. "They were very sweet and juicy. I had one at breakfast-time. I'm going to post this letter for my Mother, all by myself."

"Well, well! She must be pleased to have someone to help her like that," said the greengrocer. "You'll be coming along to my shop next, and buying cabbages and cauliflowers!"

"I might," said Betsy-May, and she felt very big again. She walked on, right down the road, and she didn't meet anyone else at all.

Betsy-May came to the tall red pillar-box. It was a lovely bright colour, and very smooth and shiny. She thought the slot for the letters was like a big mouth. She reached up with the letter.

But she wasn't tall enough to post it! She just couldn't reach. She tried and she tried, and twice the letter fell down to the ground. Betsy-May picked it up and dusted it.

She was very upset. It was dreadful to be sent to post a letter and not to be able to reach. She had felt so big – and everyone had told her she was big– but she wasn't even big enough to put the letter into the red pillar-box.

"What shall I do?" thought Betsy-May. "I can't go home again with the letter. Mother and Nanny will think I am very little. And I really don't want to ask anyone to lift me up. That's only what happens to babies."

She stood there and stood there. She was so disappointed that she felt she might cry at any moment. But it would be babyish to cry.

Nearby was a little cottage with blue curtains. Betsy-May knew who lived there. It was Mr. Frost. He walked with a stick and he always smiled at her when he saw her.

Suddenly the gate of the little cottage clicked, and Betsy-May turned round. It was Mr. Frost, coming through the gate, tap-tapping with his stick.

"Good afternoon, Betsy-May," he said. "I see you have come out to post a letter. You must be growing very big."

"Well, I am," said Betsy-May. "But I can't reach the letter-box to put the letter in. And I don't want to be lifted up like a baby. I don't know what to do."

"Now, let me think," said Mr. Frost, and he tapped two or three times with his stick. "It is no use *me* posting it for you, because *you* have come out to post it. And I can cer-

tainly see that it would be babyish to be lifted up. Well —
there is only one thing to be done."

"Tell me what it is," said Betsy-May.

"I have a wooden box inside my garden," said Mr. Frost.
"If I brought it out and you stood on it, you could easily
reach the letter-box."

"Oh, thank you!" said Betsy-May. "That's a very good
idea!"

Mr. Frost went into his garden and brought out a small,
strong box. He put it by the pillar-box. Betsy-May climbed
up on it, and posted the letter quite easily!

"Thank you very much!" she said. "I am so pleased I
have posted the letter. Here is your box."

"I will keep it just inside my garden," said Mr. Frost.
"And when you come along to post a letter another time,
slip in at my gate and get the box. Then you will always be
able to post your letters, Betsy-May."

"Thank you," said Betsy-May "I daresay I may have
grown big enough to reach next time. But if I haven't I
will get your box."

"Good-bye," said Mr. Frost, and he went one way and
Betsy-May went the other; Mr. Frost's stick went tap-tap-
tap, and Betsy-May's feet went patter-patter-patter.

Betsy-May ran in at her front gate and there were Mother
and Nanny watching for her.

"I posted the letter, I posted the letter!" cried Betsy-May.
"And oh, I *did* have a lot of adventures!"

BETSY-MAY AND THE PUPPY-DOG

One day it was very fine and sunny. Betsy-May had cleaned her doll's pram till it shone beautifully, and now she wanted to take her doll for a walk.

"Nanny, I want to go out for a walk," she said. But Nanny was washing, and she shook her head.

"I'm busy, Betsy-May," she said. "I have all your dirty frocks and socks to wash. Play in the garden."

But Betsy-May still wanted to go out for a walk with her clean doll's pram so she went to find her Mother.

"Mother, I want to go out for a walk," she said. But Mother was busy too.

"I am mending your coat," she said. "You can play in the garden."

"But, Mother, my doll does so badly want to go into the lane for a walk," said Betsy-May.

"Well, listen," said Mother. "You may take your doll down the back garden, and open the gate in the wall at the bottom. You may take your pram into the lane and walk down to the pond and back. No cars come there so you will be safe. But I trust you to be careful and to come back as soon as you get to the pond."

Betsy-May was excited. She liked the little lane, because once she had seen two rabbits there. So she put on her hat and her coat, and went to her pram. Down the garden she walked, feeling rather grand because she was taking her pram out just like Nannies take out their babies.

She opened the green door in the wall, and stepped out into the lane. She walked carefully along, singing to her doll. Then an idea came into her head.

"Angela, you have been very good," she said. "You may sit up for a little while, in case we see a rabbit."

Betsy-May leaned over her pram and pulled back the covers. And, do you know, the pram was empty! There was no doll there!

Betsy-May stared in astonishment. And then she knew what had happened. She had been so excited about walking in the lane by herself that she had forgotten to put her doll into the pram. Well, well, well!

Betsy-May was very upset. It was silly to wheel a pram out without a doll in it. What would people say if they peeped into the pram and saw no baby there? They would think she was a very silly little girl.

She went rather red. She wished she had a doll. It did seem so silly to wheel the pram when it was quite empty.

She was nearly at the little green pond. Suddenly Betsy-May heard a whine and she looked towards the hedge.

She saw a very small puppy-dog there, with a little waggy tail. He stared at Betsy-May and she stared at him.

"What's the matter, puppy-dog?" said Betsy-May.

"Woof!" said the little dog, sadly.

"Are you lost?" asked Betsy-May, for she knew how horrid it is to be lost.

"Woof," answered the puppy-dog, and he drooped his little brown head.

"Well, if you are lost, come with me, and I will take you home to my Mother," said Betsy-May. "Then she will find out where you belong to."

"Woof," said the puppy-dog, but he stayed where he was. Nothing that Betsy-May could say made any difference. He was afraid of leaving the hedge.

Then Betsy-May had a lovely idea. "I'll put you in my empty pram and wheel you home to Mother!" she said. "Come along, you poor little lost puppy."

She lifted up the tiny puppy and put him into her pram.

12

His head lay on the white pillow. It did look sweet. Betsy-May covered him up with the rug. He lay there just like a doll, and looked at Betsy-May. He was very tired and cold and frightened.

Betsy-May made nice little noises as she tucked him up, just as Nanny made to other people's babies. Then she turned her pram round and wheeled it home.

She wheeled it up the garden. Mother and Nanny were there, talking over the wall to the lady next door.

"Mother! Nanny! Look at the baby in my pram!" cried Betsy-May. "I went out without my doll, and I was very upset. But it was a good thing I did because I found another baby that wanted taking care of! Look!"

Mother and Nanny looked into the pram. When they saw the little puppy there, lying half-asleep, they *were* surprised.

"Betsy-May! Whatever will you do next!" said Nanny. "Your really are a comical little thing! Look! She's got a puppy there!"

"It must be the one that Mrs. Gilbert has lost!" said

Mother, and she took it carefully out of the pram. "Betsy-May, Mrs. Gilbert, our neighbour, was just telling me that her new puppy had run away. I wonder if this is her puppy."

Do you know, it was! Mrs. Gilbert was *so* pleased! She took the puppy and cuddled it.

"Thank you very much, Betsy-May," she said. "You are a very kind little girl. Perhaps you would like to take the puppy for a walk in your pram another day. He did seem to be happy there, didn't he?"

So now each morning Betsy-May calls for Mrs. Gilbert's puppy-dog with her pram. And sometimes he lies quietly in it, and sometimes he doesn't. But Betsy-May doesn't mind, for she loves him very much.

BETSY-MAY HAS A BIRD-TABLE

When the winter came, it was very cold. Betsy-May had a woolly scarf, leggings and gloves, besides her coat and hat when she went out.

The little wild birds didn't like the cold. "Chirrup!" said the sparrows. "There isn't much to eat!"

"Tirry-lee!" said the robins, "The ground is so hard that we can't find a worm!"

The little tits were hungry too, and the big blackbirds and thrushes. And one morning a red robin went to Betsy-May's window and pecked on it with his beak.

"Tap-tap-tap! Tap-tap-tap!"

"Look, Betsy-May!" said Nanny. "There is the robin! He wants you to hurry up and give him your crumbs."

Every day Betsy-May shook out her crumbs on the window-sill. She threw them out to the robin – but when she saw all the hungry birds sitting in the trees around, she was sad.

"Nanny, I've only got a few crumbs to give the birds," she said. "And there are *so* many birds waiting. What shall we do? I don't like them to be hungry and cold."

"Well, wouldn't it be fun to have a bird-table!" said Nanny. "We will ask Gardener to make one for you. Then we will get all the bits from Cook each day and you shall put them on the table for the birds. What a feast they will have!"

Gardener said he could easily make the table. Betsy-May watched him. He took an old broom-handle, and on to it he nailed a flat piece of wood. Then he carried it to the piece of garden outside the nursery window and stuck the handle fast into the ground.

"Oh, it's a tall one-legged table!" said Betsy-May in delight. "Oh, won't the birds be pleased. Nanny! Nanny! Come and see!"

Nanny and Mother came to see. They were pleased. Mother found an old saucer and filled it with water.

"The birds can drink this," she said.

"Perhaps they will have a bath in it too!" said Betsy-May. "I once saw the robin splashing in the puppy-dog's water next door."

Every morning Betsy-May put out all her crumbs on the table. She scraped out the milk-pudding bits and put those on the table too. Once Cook gave her a whole potato baked in its jacket and Betsy-May put it on the table. You should have seen how the thrushes pecked at it! They were so delighted.

"We must collect berries for our bird-table when we go out for our walks," said Nanny. "That will be fun."

So Betsy-May looked out for hips and haws, and once she found a great many purple privet berries too. She collected the pink, jelly-like berries of the yew, because she knew that the thrushes and blackbirds loved these.

"I mustn't eat these berries myself, must I, Nanny?" she said. "They would make me ill."

"You must only eat blackberries," said Nanny. "Look – there are some thistles going to seed in the hedge. The finches will like them. Shake the seeds into this envelope and we will put them on the table too."

So Betsy-May had a great many things to put on the bird-table for her wild birds. And dear me, didn't they love everything!

"Chirrup!" said the sparrows. "We like the seeds and the crumbs and the potato!"

"Tirry-lee!" said the robins. "We like the crumbs and the milk-pudding bits!"

"Tweet-sweet-tweet!" said the blackbirds and thrushes. "We do like the berries and the potatoes."

"Pimm-im-im-im-im!" said the little tits. "What's for us, what's for us?"

"What can we give the little green and yellow tits?" asked Betsy-May.

"Would you like to buy them a coco-nut?" said Nanny. "They love that."

So Betsy-May bought a coco-nut and the gardener broke

it in half for her. She hung the halves from the table – and then how she loved to watch the little tits swinging on the nuts all day long, pecking away hard! They were so pleased!

"Betsy-May, here is a bone for your birds," said Cook, one day, and she gave Betsy-May a big bone.

"Do birds like bones?" said Betsy-May, surprised. She hung it up and do you know, the tits flew to it, and the greedy starlings tried their hardest to perch on it too! It was such fun to watch them all.

Sometimes the robins bathed in their drinking-water, and made a great splashing. That made Betsy-May laugh. She laughed when the starlings quarrelled too, and tried to push each other off the hanging bone.

"Oh, I do like my bird-table," said Betsy-May. "It's just as good as a toy. Mother, are the birds pleased because I have a table specially for them?"

"Of course they are," said Mother. "And they will give you your reward in the spring-time, Betsy-May. You will hear them singing merrily to you from morning to night then! That is their way of saying thank you."

I expect you would like to have a bird-table too, wouldn't you? It is such fun to feed the little wild birds and watch them. You must make one too, and then, like Betsy-May, you will have the birds singing thank you in your garden all the spring-time through!

WHEN BETSY-MAY GOT LOST

Betsy-May loved puppies and kittens and ducklings – but most of all she loved puppies!

"I wish I could have a puppy of my own," she told Mummy.

"Oh, they make the house so dirty," said Mummy, "and Nanny has quite enough to do looking after you, without having to manage a puppy as well."

"I've never had anything to do with dogs," said Nanny, "and I don't think I'd like one in the nursery. He would chew your toys to bits, Betsy-May, and he would eat my slippers."

Betsy-May thought it would be fun to have a dog that ate people's slippers, but she didn't say so. She just wished again that she could have any sort of a dog.

One day, on Betsy-May's sixth birthday, Mummy said she would take her to Mrs. Field's farm, for a treat.

"It shall be your birthday treat," she said. "Mrs. Field wrote to say that she had some baby lambs and three little calves, lots of yellow ducklings and tiny chicks, and if I would take you, she would like to show you them all."

Betsy-May thought that was perfectly lovely. "All the things I love," she said. "Oh yes, Mummy, do let's go. But Nanny must go too. I must have her on my birthday as well."

"Of course," said Mummy. "Nanny, will you be ready in half an hour? I will get out the car and we will soon be there."

So Nanny put on Betsy-May's new blue jersey, and made her neat and tidy. She took mackintoshes in case it rained,

19

and a book to read to Betsy-May in the car, if she didn't want to look out of the window.

It wasn't very far to the farm. Betsy-May jumped out, and danced round in joy. The sun was shining. The farmhouse looked cosy and friendly. Sheep were baa-ing in the meadows and tiny lambs were frisking all about their big grey mothers.

"First we must go and say How-do-you-do to Mrs. Field," said Mummy. "Come along! Then you can go and see everything."

So they went to see Mrs. Field, and she hugged Betsy-May and gave her a ginger-snap biscuit to eat and said: "Many happy returns of the day!"

Mummy and Nanny sat down in Mrs. Field's beautiful parlour to have a cup of tea. Betsy-May couldn't sit down and wait for them.

"I want to go out," she said.

"Well, run along," said Mummy. "Keep away from the pond and you'll be all right. Go and see the lambs and the calves."

Betsy-May rushed out into the garden, eating her biscuit. She wondered where to go first. Then she heard the cheeping of dozens of tiny chicks and she ran to where they scampered around a big wooden coop. In the coop was their mother-hen, and when she saw Betsy-May she said "Cluck, cluck, cluck!" in an angry voice. All the little chicks rushed to her at once and hid under her feathers.

"Oh, please come out again!" cried Betsy-May. "I won't hurt you."

So after a bit they all came out again, and ran round Betsy-May's feet, calling "Cheep, cheep, cheep" in little high voices.

"Now I shall go and see the lambs," said Betsy-May. But on the way she passed a shed, and inside the shed she could hear a noise of somebody crying.

"Ooo, ooo ooo!" said the voice. "Ooo, ooo, ooo!"

Betsy-May put her eyes to a crack in the door and peeped inside to see who was making the noise. And just by the door, scratching hard at it and yelping, was a small fat puppy. It was brown and white, and was trying its hardest to get out.

"Oh!" said Betsy-May. "Have they shut you up on this beautiful fine day? What a shame! Don't tell anyone if I let you out for a little while, Puppy."

"Ooo, ooo, ooo!" said the puppy, and scraped at the door again. Betsy-May slipped down the latch and the wooden door swung open. Out leapt the puppy and danced all round her in joy. Betsy-May loved him. She bent down and picked him up. He lay quite still in her arms, a fat, warm, cosy lump. His red tongue flicked out and kissed her nose.

"Oh, you do feel lovely!" cried Betsy-May. "I wish you were mine. I should call you Tubby because you are so round and fat."

The puppy struggled to get down. Betsy-May put him gently on the ground. "You can just run round the grass and back," she said. "Then I must put you in the shed again." But the puppy ran right away.

He ran to the gate. He slipped under it. He tore over the field at top speed. Betsy-May ran after him in dismay.

"Puppy! Puppy! Come back at once! You'll get lost! Oh, Puppy, do come back!"

But the puppy wanted to go the wood and look for a rabbit. So he tore across the field and disappeared into the wood. Betsy-May tore after him. Her fat legs didn't go as fast as the puppy's, but it didn't take her long to reach the wood. She stood between the trees and shouted:

"Puppy! Puppy! Come back to me!"

"Wuff, wuff!" said the puppy, in a doggy little voice. He peeped at Betsy-May behind a bush. She rushed at him. He ran away. Betsy-May panted after him, going deeper and deeper into the wood.

And at last she caught the puppy. She held him tight in her arms, and he wuffed and wriggled, but it wasn't any use, she wouldn't let him go.

"You'll just go home with *me*," she said. She walked a few steps through the cool green wood and then she stopped. There was no path to follow!

"How can I go back to the farm if there isn't a path!" said Betsy-May, and she felt frightened. "I'm lost!"

"Wuff!" said the puppy, and he struggled so hard to get down that his claws hurt Betsy-May and she had to let him go. He ran round a tree, and then looked back at Betsy-May, as if he didn't like to leave her.

"You needn't think I'm going to follow you even deeper into the wood!" said Betsy-May, almost in tears. "Because I'm not! You've lost me! I don't know where I am and nobody else does either."

She was tired with all her running, and she sat down under a birch tree. She thought perhaps she would soon hear Mummy calling to her. But nobody came at all, and nobody called. The puppy was gone. Only a small rabbit came and peeped at Betsy-May, and wondered why she had tears running down her cheeks.

The puppy ran all the way back home. By the time he got there, Mummy and Nanny were looking for Betsy-May and calling for her. "Betsy-May! Betsy-May! Where are you?"

"Oh dear!" said Nanny. "I didn't really like her going off like that by herself. I wish I'd gone with her. Betsy-May! Betsy-May!"

But Betsy-May was too far off to hear. Then Mrs. Field saw the puppy running round loose and she was surprised. "Look!" she said. "There's the puppy loose. Do you think Betsy-May let him out? If she did, he would tear off to the woods, as he always does – and Betsy-May might have gone after him and got lost!"

"Oh dear – let's go to the woods then," said Mummy. So they all set off for the wood – the puppy-dog too. And as soon as they got there, the puppy remembered poor Betsy-May and he rushed off to find her. He remembered exactly where he had left her.

Betsy-May was still sitting under the birch tree, feeling very sad. Suddenly the puppy came round a tree and flung

himself on her. Betsy-May was *so* pleased to see him. She cuddled him and loved him, and he licked her chin till it was very wet.

Then he wriggled out of her arms, stood by her, and began to bark in his puppy-dog voice. "Wuff! Wuff! Wuff!"

That was to make Mummy and Nanny and Mrs. Field hear him and come to him to find Betsy-May. They did hear him, and they hurried towards his voice. Nanny called loudly as she went: "Betsy-May! Betsy-May!"

"I'm here! I'm here!" shouted Betsy-May. "The puppy has got me. Here I am!"

And then Mummy, Nanny, and Mrs. Field came round a tree, and saw Betsy-May and the good little puppy standing close beside her, barking for all he was worth to tell them he had found Betsy-May! How they hugged one another! The puppy ran all round them, as happy as could be.

"Isn't he a clever puppy?" said Betsy-May, picking him up to carry him home. "I do love him. I wish he was mine."

"Well, would you like him for a birthday present?" asked Mrs. Field. "He has already looked after you well, Betsy-May, and I am sure he would be glad if he could be your dog and look after you always."

And Mummy said yes! Betsy-May could hardly believe her ears. "Yes," said Mummy. "I really think we'll have him, Mrs. Field. I think a dog would be a good companion for Betsy-May – especially if she is going to get lost like this."

So they took him home with them at the end of the day, fast asleep in Betsy-May's arms. "He's my nicest present," she said. "My own little puppy-dog, Tubby. Oh, I am so happy! Won't it be lovely to wake up to-morrow morning and remember that I've got a puppy-dog of my very, very own!"

BETSY-MAY AT THE SEASIDE

Betsy-May was at the seaside for two weeks. It was simply lovely! There was sand everywhere on the beach – dry sand, wet sand, sand to build up into castles, and sand to dig into holes.

Tubby, Betsy-May's mad little puppy, was with her too,

and when Betsy-May dug, *he* dug! He dug with his paws, not with a spade, but he managed to make just as deep a hole as Betsy-May did! He sent the sand flying high into the air, and Nanny didn't like it at all when he covered her with sand.

Betsy-May and Nanny were alone. Mummy and Daddy had gone for a holiday by themselves. Nanny, Betsy-May, and Tubby were in a dear little house by the beach, looked after by nice, kind Mrs. Brown.

The only thing Mrs. Brown didn't like about having Nanny and Betsy-May, was Tubby. She wasn't used to dogs. She said they were dirty, noisy, and quite mad. And, indeed, it seemed as if she was right, because Tubby was always walking over her clean hall with dirty paws, he barked whenever anyone came to the door, and he often went quite mad.

Then he would race round and round the room and knock everything over. Betsy-May thought he was lovely when he did that – but Nanny and Mrs. Brown were very cross with him.

"I wish we hadn't brought Tubby," said Nanny. "I wish we had left him behind with Biddle, the gardener."

"Oh, Nanny! I couldn't bear to leave Tubby behind," said Betsy-May, who loved her puppy very much indeed. "He does mean to be good, I'm sure he does."

It didn't really seem as if Tubby meant to be good. He went into the kitchen one day, when Mrs. Brown was out in the garden hanging up clothes. He smelt a nice smell and he jumped up on the table to see if he could find it.

The smell came from a steak-and-kidney pie that Mrs. Brown had cooked for dinner. Tubby didn't wait to ask whose dinner it was! He made it his own dinner at once!

He gobbled down that pie – crust and all – and then went to lie down in his basket, feeling very full-up and happy. But he wasn't happy long.

When Mrs. Brown found out what he had done, she was so angry that Betsy-May was quite frightened.

"And now we'll just have to have sardines for dinner," she said. "That dog ought to have a good whipping."

"Oh no!" said Betsy-May, nearly in tears. "You mustn't whip him. He's mine."

"Well, he must certainly have a good smacking," said Nanny. She took Tubby firmly by his collar and led him to the kitchen. She showed him the empty pie-dish and then she smacked him very hard four times. Tubby yelped and cried, and rushed out into the garden. Betsy-May was very unhappy.

She talked to Tubby a long time that afternoon, and told him that he really must be good. "You see, you are in some one else's house," she said, "and so you must be extra well-behaved. You don't want to be sent back home to Biddle, do you, Tubby?"

"Wuff, wuff!" said Tubby, and he licked Betsy-May's cheek till she pushed him away.

Tubby was good for the rest of that day – and then he did another dreadful thing. He found Mrs. Brown's old blue bedroom-slippers under her bed, and took them down to the beach. And when Mrs. Brown came down to the beach to have a little chat with Nanny, what did she see but her old bedroom-slippers lying there on the sand, with Tubby chewing the toes!

"Look at that!" said Mrs. Brown, going red with rage.

"What?" asked Nanny, looking up from her knitting. "Oh! I can't think where Tubby found those dreadful old bedroom-slippers. Some one must have thrown them away on the beach, I suppose."

"Those are *my* bedroom-slippers," said Mrs. Brown in a very angry voice. "They are not dreadful at all. They are very cosy and comfortable – and now that dog of yours is eating them for his dinner!"

Betsy-May was very upset. She drove away Tubby, picked up the slippers and slapped them together to get the sand out. Both the toes were chewed into holes.

"Please, Mrs. Brown, I will buy you some nice new ones," said Betsy-May. "Daddy gave me some money to spend on ice-creams, but I will spend it on new slippers for you."

"You're a kind little girl," said Mrs. Brown; "but you needn't bother to do that. I've a new pair some one gave me at Christmas. It's just that those old ones were so *very* comfortable. You will have to smack Tubby very hard."

"Oh, I will," promised Betsy-May. "I'll smack him when we get home. I don't like to smack him in front of all the other dogs here. He might feel so ashamed."

"And a good thing too," said Mrs. Brown.

Betsy-May did smack Tubby when they got home, but it wasn't much of a smacking. Tubby really thought it was an extra nice patting, and he was very pleased. He wagged his little tail hard and licked Betsy-May on the nose.

"Now, please, please, don't do anything else," said Betsy-May. "Mrs. Brown is such a nice kind person, Tubby."

"Wuff!" said Tubby, and he sat down, cocked one ear up at Betsy-May, and looked too good for words. Betsy-May was quite sure he wouldn't do anything else naughty at all.

But she was wrong. Whatever do you think he did on Mrs. Brown's washing-day? He saw the clothes flapping in the wind, and jumped at a petticoat on the line. He caught it in his sharp little teeth and tugged hard. Down came the line! Tubby was pleased and excited. He tugged and tugged at the line of clothes. The rope wasn't very strong and it broke. Tubby tore down to the beach, with the line of clothes galloping behind him.

"Wuff, wuff! Look what *I've* caught!" he barked. "Just look! Wuff, wuff!"

Nanny, Betsy-May, and Mrs. Brown looked, and all together they sprang to their feet, rushed at Tubby, and caught hold of the line of clothes that was dragging in the sand. Nanny spanked Tubby till he cried. Mrs. Brown gathered up her clothes, and said one dreadful sentence:

"That dog must be sent home."

She went up to her cottage with the clothes. Nanny looked at Betsy-May. "I'm afraid he *will* have to go home," she said. "He is really very, very naughty, Betsy-May."

"Yes – he is," said Betsy-May sadly. "But I shall be *so* lonely without him! Oh, Tubby, why are you such a naughty little dog?"

Tubby was angry and hurt because he had been smacked. He ran off to paddle in the sea. He wouldn't look at Nanny or Betsy-May. He paddled so far out that he had to swim. But he liked that. He bobbed up and down, swimming with all his four fat legs.

Betsy-May couldn't help thinking that he was very clever. She couldn't swim at all herself, except in the bath at home, and she knew that wasn't real swimming.

"Perhaps you will arrange for the dog to go back on Monday," said Mrs. Brown that day. "To-morrow is Sunday, and the trains are bad – but you could give him to the guard on Monday, and he will be all right till he gets to your station. Your gardener could meet the train and take him home."

Betsy-May cried. Nanny gave her a long curly piece of barley-sugar to comfort her, but her tears ran on to it and made the barley-sugar taste salt. So Betsy-May gave it to Tubby, and he crunched it up in half a second.

The next day was Sunday, and Mrs. Brown said she was going to church. "I'll come and sit on the beach with you for a few minutes when I come out of church," she said. "I'm just going to get ready now."

When she came downstairs, Betsy-May cried out in surprise: "Oh! What a beautiful hat, Mrs. Brown! It's the loveliest one in the world!"

Mrs. Brown was pleased. *She* thought her new hat was beautiful too. It was blue, and all around it were mixed flowers – cornflowers, daisies, roses, buttercups, sweet-peas – really, it was like a little garden.

"Oh, I wish *I* had a hat like that," said Betsy-May. "Oh, I do wish I had. You do look so nice, Mrs. Brown."

"Yes, it certainly suits you," said Nanny. Mrs. Brown was proud and pleased. She smiled at them and went off to church in her new hat.

After church, she came down to the beach as she had

promised. It was very windy. Mrs. Brown held on tightly to her new hat. But she had to let go to catch at her scarf which the wind was trying to blow away.

And her hat flew right off her head up into the air! It rushed up into the breeze, a mass of bright flowers, and then fell down to the sand and began to roll away fast.

"My new hat!" cried Mrs. Brown. "Oh, my best new hat! Oh dear, oh dear, oh dear!"

She sounded as if she was going to cry. It was dreadful. Nanny jumped to her feet, but the new hat was too far away for her to catch. Betsy-May felt upset. She had so liked Mrs. Brown's flower-hat.

"It'll blow into the sea! It'll be spoilt!" said Mrs. Brown sadly.

But who was this after the hat, scampering on four quick legs over the sand, wuffing loudly? It was Tubby! "I'll catch you, I'll catch you!" he cried. "What, you think you can race me! Rubbish!"

The hat rolled away fast, down to the edge of the sea. It jumped cleverly over a puddle. Tubby wasn't so clever. He went splash into the middle of the puddle. He splashed out, and raced after the rolling hat. And just as it got to the edge of the sea, he caught it!

He snapped at it – and there it was, quite still in his mouth.

"Tubby, Tubby, come here!" shouted Betsy-May. "Oh, you clever dog! Oh, you good dog! Bring it here, bring it here!"

So Tubby proudly ran back, carrying the hat very carefully. It wasn't spoilt a bit, except that it was sandy round the edges.

"Thank you, Tubby," said Mrs. Brown, and she patted him. "You are very good. I won't send you home tomorrow after all."

So Tubby stayed at the seaside till they all went home;

and do you know, he was as good as gold after that. Betsy-May was so happy.

"He'll always be good now, Nanny," she said. "You'll see, he'll *always* be good."

But Nanny didn't think so!

BETSY-MAY AND OLD MRS. JENKS

Sometimes when Nanny, Tubby, and Betsy-May went out for their afternoon walk they passed old Mrs. Jenks's house.

Betsy-May always tried to hurry by quickly, because she didn't like old Mrs. Jenks. She was afraid of her because she looked ugly.

Mrs. Jenks wore glasses that made her eyes look simply enormous. They seemed to glare at Betsy-May, and Betsy-May didn't like it.

Then Mrs. Jenks had funny hands. They were knobbly and twisted. Nanny said Mrs. Jenks had had something called rheumatism, and that had made her hands queer.

"I wish she'd have them put right, then," said Betsy-May. "I don't like looking at them."

"Well, don't look at them then," said Nanny.

"If I don't look at her hands I have to look at her face, and I don't like Mrs. Jenks's glaring sort of eyes," said Betsy-May.

"Oh, you're too fussy altogether," said Nanny.

Mrs. Jenks didn't like dogs at all. She said they came and scraped up her garden. She was proud of her little garden, and indeed it was very lovely and gay. It had the first clumps of snowdrops in the village, and when it was crocus-time her garden was purple and golden all over. In March it was yellow with daffodils.

All the year round it was lovely and Betsy-May liked to lean over the little fence and look at it whenever she passed by. But she always kept a sharp lookout for Mrs. Jenks, and if she saw her anywhere about, Betsy-May would hurry by and not give the flowers the tiniest look.

Once she had seen Mrs. Jenks in a great temper, chasing Mr. Frost's dog out of her garden with a stick. She had given the dog a big whack, and it had cried and yelped.

"Mrs. Jenks is a horrid woman," Betsy-May told Nanny.

"You shouldn't say things like that," said Nanny. "She just feels cross because that great dog came and scraped up her lovely red tulips."

"Well, I shall go on *thinking* she is a horrid person, even if I don't say it," said Betsy-May.

"You shouldn't think unkind things *or* say them," said Nanny. "For all you know, Mrs. Jenks may be very nice indeed. She has a black cat that loves her, I know. And I've seen her feeding the birds."

"Well, she looks horrid," said Betsy-May. "Her eyes glare at me."

"I think you are being very silly, Betsy-May," said Nanny, and she wouldn't say any more.

Now one summer afternoon, when Nanny was out with Betsy-May and Tubby, they came to Mrs. Jenks's house. The garden looked lovely. It was full of roses, lilies, and sweet-peas. Betsy-May leaned over the fence and sniffed at it, and looked at it with gladness.

And then Nanny said something dreadful. "Betsy-May, just run up the garden-path and give this note to Mrs. Jenks," she said. "I must hold Tubby on the lead. I can't take him up the path in case he spoils any of the flowers. Here is the note."

"I don't want to take it," said Betsy-May, going red. "You know I don't like Mrs. Jenks, Nanny. I'll hold Tubby, and you can take it."

"Betsy-May, do as you are told, and don't be a baby," said Nanny crossly. "Hurry now – just run up the path, and slip the note into the letter box. I expect Mrs. Jenks is out."

Betsy-May hoped she was. She didn't like being called a baby, so she took the note, opened the little green gate, and ran up the path very quickly.

33

But the letter-box was very stiff, and she found it difficult to open. She tried to push it so that she could slip in the note, but it slipped from her hand, and shut itself with quite a loud noise.

And suddenly the door opened, and there stood Mrs. Jenks, with her big round glasses on, and her poor knobbly hands! Betsy-May got such a shock!

"Did you want to give me a message, dear?" said Mrs. Jenks in a soft voice. "Oh, I see – you have a note for me. Well, come in for a minute and I will read it and see if there is an answer."

"I'll wait here, please," said Betsy-May in a trembling voice.

"No, come along in," said Mrs. Jenks, and she took hold of Betsy-May's arm and pulled her indoors. Betsy-May's eyes filled with tears, and to Mrs. Jenks's alarm she saw the tears rolling down Betsy-May's cheeks.

"What's the matter?" she asked. "Why, Betsy-May – you're not afraid of me, are you?"

"Yes, I am," sobbed Betsy-May. "I don't like the way your eyes glare."

Mrs. Jenks took off her big round glasses, and looked at Betsy-May.

"Is that better?" she asked.

Betsy-May looked up at her. She saw a little round-faced person with soft brown eyes like Tubby, her puppy. The eyes were small and didn't glare at all. They were nice eyes.

"You look different," said Betsy-May.

"It's my glasses that make my eyes big and staring," said Mrs. Jenks. "But you see, Betsy-May, they don't see very well without glasses, so I just *have* to wear them. I don't like them at all. But I won't wear them when you come to see me."

"Your eyes are brown like Tubby's," said Betsy-May. "I

like them without the big glasses. Mrs. Jenks, why have you got such funny hands?"

"I had an illness," said Mrs. Jenks sadly. "Sometimes old people get it, and then our fingers go knobbly and twisted. I can't sew, my dear, and I can't knit, with my poor old hands. I can't do very much for myself or for other people either, and it makes me sad. I know little children think I am ugly, and that makes me sad too."

And quite suddenly Mrs. Jenks's old hands were not ugly any more to Betsy-May. She was sorry for them, because they couldn't sew or knit or do what they wanted to. She looked up at Mrs. Jenks's soft brown eyes and smiled.

"I don't think you are ugly," she said. "I will ask Biddle, our gardener, to give me one of his special plants for your garden. But don't wear your glasses when I come, will you?"

"No, I won't," said Mrs. Jenks. "And now, I wonder if I've got something you would like. Look along my mantel-piece, Betsy-May, and see if there is anything there you would like for a present from me."

Betsy-May looked. There were most exciting things on

Mrs. Jenks's mantelpiece. There was a tiny china cottage with a door, two windows, and a chimney. There was a small man who sat and nodded his head when it was touched. There was a little woman who rocked when you pushed her, but wouldn't fall down. And there were two china cats with long pink tongues curling out of their mouths.

"Can I really have one of them?" asked Betsy-May. "Well – I'd simply love that little man who nods his head, Mrs. Jenks. Are you sure you won't miss him if I have him? I do like him so."

"He's been waiting there for you to come and take him," said Mrs. Jenks. "And now, what about a nice bone for your puppy-dog?"

"But I thought you didn't like dogs," said Betsy-May, surprised.

"I like them *out*side my garden," said Mrs. Jenks, going to her larder. "I don't like them *in*side. I'm very fond of them outside in the road."

She gave Betsy-May a nice clean bone for Tubby. "And now I will cut one of my best roses for your mother," she said. "I know she loves the kind I have growing by the window."

Mrs. Jenks's old hands couldn't cut the rose very well, so Betsy-May cut if for her, very carefully, with a nice long stalk. Then she said good-bye to Mrs. Jenks, and went happily down the path.

"I'll come again as soon as I can!" she called. "And thank you for the lovely nodding man."

"Well, good gracious me, I thought you must be spending the whole day with Mrs. Jenks," said Nanny, when Betsy-May joined her. "You made such a fuss about going to leave the note – and then you stay and stay and stay."

"Nanny, Mrs. Jenks is the kindest person in the world," said Betsy-May. "I'm sorry I thought unkind things of her now."

"I told you that Mrs. Jenks might be very nice indeed," said Nanny. "You shouldn't make up your mind that people are horrid before you know them."

"I shan't again," said Betsy-May. "Do look at my nodding man, Nanny! Ask him a question and see what he does!"

"Little nodding man, don't you think that Betsy-May is a funny little girl?" asked Nanny.

And the little man nodded and nodded and nodded!

BETSY-MAY GETS INTO TROUBLE

Nanny put on Betsy-May's garden overall and her sun-hat.

"Now you are ready to play in the garden," she said. "I shall be very busy washing this morning, so you must be good, and play nicely with Tubby. If you are as good as gold I will take you to feed the ducks in the park this afternoon."

Betsy-May loved feeding the ducks. "I shall be as good as gold and as good as silver too!" she said.

"Betsy-May, don't go into the hen-house," called Nanny, as Betsy-May ran off down the garden.

Betsy-May didn't answer. She didn't want to hear what Nanny said about the hen-house. She simply loved opening the wire-gate, creeping in among the clucking hens, and lifting up the lids of the nesting-boxes to see if any eggs were there. When she had been very good, Mummy would sometimes let her carry a warm egg in each hand to the kitchen.

It was tiresome of Nanny to say she mustn't go into the hen-house. "But I didn't really hear what she said, and I didn't answer her," thought Betsy-May to herself. "She might have said something different."

For a little while she played with Tubby, chasing him round and round a flower-bed. Then Tubby got tired and lay down on his back with all his four legs in the air. Betsy-May tickled him and then looked at the hen-house.

"Cackle-cackle-cackle!" said a hen proudly, just exactly as if she was talking to Betsy-May.

"Have you laid an egg?" asked Betsy-May.

"Cluck-a-luck-a-cluck!" answered the hen, her head on one side, looking at Betsy-May through the wire.

"That means you've laid one, I know it does," said Betsy-May. "Is it brown or white? I want a brown one for my breakfast. Did you know that brown eggs always taste nicer than white ones, hen?"

"Cuck, cu-u-u-u-uck!" said the hen, and ran off to jump up at the cabbage stalk that hung in the middle of the run.

"I do wonder if the egg is brown or white, Tubby," said Betsy-May to the puppy. Tubby didn't care which it was. He rolled over, shut his eyes, and suddenly fell fast asleep in the hot sun.

"You always go to sleep when I want to talk to you, Tubby," said Betsy-May. "I *do* want to know if that egg is white or brown."

She wanted to know so badly that at last she got up and went to the hen-run. All the hens were clucking to one another and scratching up the ground.

"I can't see that it would matter if I went to look at that egg," thought Betsy-May. "After all, I didn't say I wouldn't go. I'll just slip in quickly, and then out again. It can't matter and no one will know."

So she undid the gate and went in. She shut the gate behind her. She ran to the nesting-boxes and lifted up one lid after another. There was a beautiful big brown egg in the last box of all.

"Oh! Isn't it lovely!" said Betsy-May to the hens. "I wonder if it's warm."

Betsy-May loved holding warm eggs in her hand. She picked up the egg and held it. It was as warm as toast and felt delicious.

Suddenly one of the hens pecked Betsy-May's leg. She had a brown freckle on it, and the hen thought it was a fly. So she pecked hard. Betsy-May gave a squeal – and dropped the brown egg!

It broke on the ground! The yellow yolk flowed out and

made a little puddle. Betsy-May stood and looked at it in horror. She had broken that lovely egg.

She knelt down to pick up the shell, and somehow or other she got egg on her clean overall. There it was, a bright yellow stain. Now Nanny would know she had been into the hen-house and broken an egg.

"I don't want her to know," said Betsy-May. "I will wash my overall in front and wipe up the broken egg."

She ran out of the hen-run to get something to wipe up the egg. On the clothes-line there was a white cloth. Betsy-May unpegged it.

"I can wash it when I wash my overall," she said. She went back to the hen-run – but alas! Betsy-May had left the gate open, and now all the hens were wandering over the garden!

"Oh dear, what a bother!" said Betsy-May. She mopped up the broken egg with the cloth. It made it very dirty, because she mopped up some of the dusty earth, too.

"I'd better wash my overall before I shoo back the hens," thought Betsy-May. "Oh dear! – why did I go to the hen-house? I do wish I hadn't!"

She ran to the greenhouse to get some water from the tank there to wash her overall in front.

"I'll dip a can into the water and fill it," said Betsy-May. So she dipped in the can and filled it. She tried to put it up on the shelf above the tank, but it was so heavy that she couldn't do it properly. The can fell forward, soaked her with water, and then crashed down on to some pots of plants below.

"Oh dear!" said Betsy-May. She stood and stared. Three pots were broken, and the plants were spoilt. Her overall, shoes, and stockings were soaking wet. Now what was she to do?

Suddenly she heard Mummy's voice calling to the gardener.

"Biddle! Biddle! The hens are out! They are scraping up all your new seedlings."

Then Biddle, Mummy, and Nanny all tore round the garden after the hens, who had scraped up about fifty of Biddle's nice little seedlings. Betsy-May stood at the door of the greenhouse, crying.

Mummy saw her and stopped chasing the hens. "What's the matter, Betsy-May?" she called.

"I'm wet!" sobbed Betsy-May.

Mummy came up, surprised. She saw Betsy-May's wet shoes and socks and overall.

"Whatever have you been doing?" she asked. "Was it you who let the hens out, Betsy-May?"

"Yes. I left the gate open," said poor Betsy-May.

Nanny came up just then, and she frowned.

"Oh, Betsy-May! I told you not to go into the hen-run. Did you disobey?"

"Yes," wept Betsy-May. "I went to see if a hen had laid an egg for me, and it had. And one of the hens pecked my leg and made me drop the egg. And it broke. And I took that cloth off the line to wipe up the mess."

"My best cloth!" said Mummy.

"And I left the gate open by mistake and all the hens got out," sobbed Betsy-May. "And I filled the can to wash your cloth and my overall, and it fell all over me and broke these plants, and wetted me like this."

"You'd better go indoors with Nanny and let her dry you and clean you up," said Mummy in a stern voice. "I am not pleased with you."

So Betsy-May was taken to the bathroom. Her shoes and socks were taken off and her feet were dried. Her overall was taken off and another one put on. Nanny put the dirty one into the bath to wash, and Mummy's cloth, too.

"Nanny, I only just went into the hen-house," said

Betsy-May. "I didn't know all these dreadful things were going to happen."

"Now listen to me, Betsy-May," said Nanny in a very cross voice. "If you do one little thing you are not supposed to do, it may quite well turn into a whole lot of big things that will give you a nasty surprise. You didn't think it

mattered going into the hen-house when you were told not to – but see what has happened! You broke a nice egg. You spoilt Mummy's best cloth. You messed your overall. You let all the hens escape. Biddle's new seedlings are all eaten. Your shoes and socks are soaked – and you have broken three of Biddle's nicest greenhouse plants! And all because you were silly enough to do what you were told not to!"

"It's really dreadful, Nanny, isn't it?" said Betsy-May, a tear trickling down her nose.

"It is," said Nanny. "Now I shall have to do some more washing, as you see, so I shall not have time to take you to feed the ducks this afternoon. And I'm afraid you will have to go without your breakfast egg, because you have broken the one that the hen laid for your breakfast."

"All right, Nanny," said Betsy-May, wiping her tears

42

away. "It's all my own fault. I shan't grumble. I'll be as good as gold for the rest of the day. I won't let any more little things turn into a horrid lot of big things. How *dare* they?"

"Oh, they dare every day of the week, if we let them!" said Nanny. "Now run away and play."

So Betsy-May ran out to Tubby, and for the rest of the day she really was as good as gold. She can be if she tries!

BETSY-MAY AND THE KITCHEN STOVE

Nanny had to go shopping in the village one afternoon, so Betsy-May went with her, very pleased. "Now I shall be able to look in the toy-shop window," she said. "Will you leave me outside, whilst you go shopping, Nanny, if I promise not to move?"

"We'll see," said Nanny. They set off together, with Tubby jumping round their heels, very pleased at going for a walk.

Betsy-May walked very nicely, and behaved herself very well. When they came to the village Nanny said she was going into the book-shop, next door to the toy-shop, and Betsy-May could stand and look at the toys.

"If you'll promise faithfully not to go away from the window," Nanny said.

"I promise faithfully," said Betsy-May. So Nanny went into the book-shop, and Betsy-May was left pressing her nose against the toy-shop window.

It was a lovely window, the nicest in the whole village. At the back were three big dolls – one a baby doll, one a boy doll, and one a girl doll. The boy doll had a little dog by him on a lead, and it was very like Tubby. Betsy-May lifted her puppy up to see it.

There were two boats and a ship, a railway with an engine and three carriages on the rails, a fine tunnel, a signal, and a station with little people standing on the platform.

Betsy-May stood and looked and looked. She looked into every single corner of the window – and then, tucked away at the back, she saw something simply lovely. It was a tiny dolls'-house stove!

Now Betsy-May had a dolls' house with a kitchen, a drawing-room, and two bedrooms – but there was no stove in the kitchen at all. It was a great pity – because the dolls couldn't cook any meals for themselves if they hadn't a stove.

Betsy-May looked closely at the stove. It had an oven door, a little open. The oven door had a tiny knobhandle, just like Mummy's in the scullery. At the top was a tiny rack to put wet plates in.

"The dolls could use that when they wash up," thought Betsy-May to herself. "They could put their tiny wet plates in there to dry. How nice the little stove would look in my dolls' house! Oh, I do wish I had it!"

Nanny came out of the book-shop at that minute, and Betsy-May showed her the stove. "How much do you think it is, Nanny?" asked Betsy-May. "I would so like it for my dolls' house. Is it a penny? I've got a penny. I could buy it."

"We'll ask Miss Gilly and see," said Nanny. So they went into the toy-shop to ask Miss Gilly how much the stove was.

Miss Gilly took it out of the window and set it on the counter for Betsy-May to see. It was perfectly lovely. Its oven door opened and shut beautifully. There was room at the top for a saucepan, a kettle, and a frying-pan. Miss Gilly put them all on for Betsy-May to see.

"They go with the stove," she said. "It costs sixpence altogether."

"Oh dear!" said Betsy-May. "I've only got a penny."

"Well, you can save the other five pennies, if you badly want the stove," said Nanny. "Come along!"

Betsy-May went out of the shop, looking backwards at the beautiful kitchen stove. She had never wanted anything so much in all her life. She had made up her mind to save up and buy it as soon as ever she could. She watched Miss Gilley put it back in its place in the window.

Betsy-May began to save up. Auntie Janet came, and

gave her a penny. That made twopence. Uncle Fred met her in the street one day and gave her another penny.

"Buy some toffees with it," he said.

"Oh, Uncle Fred, do you mind if I don't?" asked Betsy-May. "I'm saving up for a kitchen stove."

"Good gracious! Well, put my penny towards it!" said Uncle Fred, laughing. So that made threepence.

Then Daddy gave her a Saturday penny, and that was fourpence. After that no pennies seemed to come along, and Betsy-May got quite worried in case somebody else might buy the little kitchen stove.

"I wish I could *earn* a penny," she said to Nanny. "I wish I could do some work."

"Well," said Nanny, "I heard Biddle say that he wished he had somebody to help him to pull up the weeds in the crazy-paving path. Perhaps Mummy would give you a penny if you helped Biddle."

"Oh, good!" said Betsy-May, and ran to ask. Mummy said yes, of course she would; so all that morning Betsy-May helped Biddle to weed the path. It was very hard work, and her fingers were tired. But she was full of joy when Mummy gave her a bright new penny for her work.

"Now I only want one more penny," she said to Nanny. "I've got fivepence. Only one more penny and I can buy that stove."

Betsy-May thought and thought how she could get a penny. Then Nanny had a good idea. "I want some flowers for our nursery table," she said. "If you would pick me a bunch out of your own little garden, I would buy them for a penny."

"Oh, would you really, Nanny!" cried Betsy-May, and she ran down to her little garden. She picked cornflowers, poppies, virginia stock and candytuft. She made them all into a gay little bunch and then ran back to the nursery. She arranged them in the little vase, and showed them to Nanny.

"Do you think they are worth a ha'penny or a penny?" she asked.

"Oh, a penny, I think, especially as you have arranged them so beautifully," said Nanny. She gave Betsy-May a penny – and that made sixpence! Betsy-May was delighted. "Now this afternoon we can go and buy my stove," she said. "I hope we meet Peter and his Nanny. Peter would like to come in and buy the stove with me."

They didn't meet Peter – but they met his Nanny. She was looking rather sad.

"Where's Peter?" asked Betsy-May.

"He has had an accident," said Peter's Nanny. "He climbed up a high tree and fell out of it this morning. He has hurt his head and his leg and his arm. He is in bed, feeling very sorry for himself. He has to be in bed for a whole week."

"Poor little Peter!" said Nanny. "I will buy him some sweets for you to take back to him. It is so nice to have presents when you are ill in bed."

"Thank you," said Peter's Nanny. "I've come out to buy him something myself. Poor little boy, he does feel bad. I think he would like to see Betsy-May, Nanny, if you would let her go in and see him this afternoon."

"Of course," said Nanny.

Betsy-May stood and stared at Peter's Nanny. She felt upset about poor Peter. "Is he hurting very much?" she asked.

"His head hurts him," said Peter's Nanny. "He cried and cried. He was going to the Zoo to-morrow, so he is very disappointed."

Betsy-May felt sorrier and sorrier. She wanted to give something to Peter to make him feel better. She felt her six round pennies, and gave a big sigh.

"I shall buy Peter a present," she said. "I've got sixpence. I want him to feel better."

47

"But you saved up all your pennies for the little stove," said Nanny in surprise.

"Yes, I know," said Betsy-May. "I'll have to save up again. I didn't know Peter was going to fall out of a tree."

Betsy-May went into the toy-shop, and the first thing she saw was a fine soldier on a horse. She knew at once that Peter would simply love it. It was sixpence. She bought it and took the soldier wrapped up in paper. He felt nice and knobbly. She gave all her pennies to Miss Gilly.

Then they went to Peter's house. He was in bed with a big white bandage round his poor head. He looked very white and sad. Betsy-May was sorry for him.

"I've come to see you, Peter," she said. "Did you really fall out of a high tree?"

"Yes – bang – like that!" said Peter, making his hand fall down on the sheet with a smack. "It hurt."

"Here's a present for you, Peter," said Betsy-May. "I bought it for you myself in the toy-shop. It's lovely."

Peter undid the paper, and took out the little soldier on horseback. He gazed at it with joy.

"Oh, Betsy-May! It's beautiful! Oh, what a lovely soldier!" cried Peter. "Oh, it's just what I wanted. Now I shall be happy all the day, with my dear little soldier to gallop over my bed. You *are* a kind girl!"

Betsy-May felt happy too. She felt all warm inside. She was glad she had spent her pennies on Peter.

She stayed with him for half an hour, and then Nanny said she must go. Just as she was going Peter called her back.

"Betsy-May! Wait a minute. I've got something for *you*! It's something that my Auntie Ellen sent me to-day, and I don't like it because I'm a boy, not a girl. Look – here it is. You have it."

And Peter held out to Betsy-May a tiny kitchen stove, with a little kettle, frying-pan, and saucepan on top! Betsy-May stared and stared. She really couldn't believe her eyes.

"Well, well, well!" said Nanny, pleased. "You spent all your kitchen stove pennies on a soldier for Peter – and now he's got the very stove you wanted, and he's giving it to you! Take it, Betsy-May darling. You deserve it."

So Betsy-May took it, and in great joy carried it home. Now it is in the kitchen of her dolls' house and looks perfectly lovely. Betsy-May is sure the dolls cook on it every single night.

BETSY-MAY AND THE PENNY

One day Betsy-May asked Nanny if she could have a penny to buy herself a big red lollipop from the sweet shop.

"You haven't any pennies in your money-box at all," said Nanny. "You spent them all last week, buying a red collar for Tubby-dog."

"I do so want a lollipop," said Betsy-May, and she made a little sulking face that nobody liked.

"Nobody wants to give lollipops to girls who make that kind of face," said Nanny at once, and she wouldn't take any more notice of Betsy-May.

Then Mummy came into the nursery with a letter to be posted. "Do you think Betsy-May would post this letter for me?" she asked. Betsy-May was simply delighted. She was allowed to post letters by herself, because it was only just down the road, and she didn't have to cross over at all.

"Yes, I'll post it, Mummy," she said. So she put on her hat, took the letter, and went down the path to the gate. She always felt very grand when she posted letters. She couldn't quite reach the mouth of the letter-box, but old Mr. Frost, who lived just nearby, kept a wooden box in his front garden, and Betsy-May knew she could borrow it to stand on. Then she could reach quite well to put the letter in.

But this morning she thought she would try to post the letter without standing on the box. So she stood on tiptoe and tried her hardest. And the letter slipped in at the red mouth, and went slithering down inside. Betsy-May had posted a letter without having to stand on Mr. Frost's box. She felt very proud.

Just as she turned to go back, she saw something lying on the ground. What do you think it was? A penny! It lay there, round and brown, and Betsy-May got such a suprise when she saw it. She picked it up and looked at it. It had a king's head on one side, and a lady with a fork the other side. It certainly was a penny.

Betsy-May was so pleased. She skipped along the pavement. "Now I shall be able to buy that red lollipop!" she thought. And then, just as she got near her gate, she saw a little boy coming along crying.

He was looking on the ground as he came, and Betsy-May knew at once what he was looking for. That penny!

"But it's mine now, it's mine," said Betsy-May to herself. "I found it. It's mine. I want to buy a red lollipop with it."

So she didn't say anything to the little boy at all. She just let him go crying along the road. She knew who he was. It was John, who lived just round the corner.

Betsy-May heard John say something as he went by. "I did want to buy a ball," he said. "I did want to buy a ball."

"And I want to buy a lollipop," said Betsy-May to herself, and she held the penny tightly. She ran indoors, and she didn't say anything about the penny at all. When Mummy came to thank her for posting the letter, she didn't even tell her that now she was tall enough to put the letter in without standing on anything.

"Would you like to come out with me?" asked Mummy. "I'm just going to the village to get some more wool."

Betsy-May put on her hat again. She trotted along by Mummy, with the brown penny still in her hot hand. When Mummy went into the wool-shop, which sold sweets as well as wool, Betsy-May spoke to Mummy. "I've got a penny," she said. "Can I buy a red lollipop, Mummy?"

"Yes, if you like," said Mummy, who was busy choosing

some wool for a new jersey for Betsy-May. So Betsy-May bought her red lollipop, and began to suck it.

Mummy soon went home again, and Betsy-May wondered where Nanny was. Somehow she didn't want her to see the red lollipop. Tubby-dog came rushing up. He smelt the red lollipop at once.

He jumped up at Betsy-May and knocked the lollipop out of her hand. Down it went on to the floor, and bits of fluff from the carpet stuck to it.

Now Betsy-May hated eating things with fluff on them, and besides, she knew it wasn't right to eat things that had fallen on the floor. So she began to cry loudly, and to scold poor Tubby. Nanny came running in to see what the matter was.

When she saw the red lollipop she was very much surprised. "Did Mummy buy it for you?" she asked.

"No, I bought it myself," said Betsy-May, wiping her eyes.

"But you didn't have any pennies," said Nanny, puzzled.

"I found one in the street when I went to post Mummy's letter," said Betsy-May.

"Why didn't you tell me that, Betsy-May?" said Nanny, still more puzzled, because usually Betsy-May told her and Mummy everything that happened. And it was exciting to find something – so how strange it was that Betsy-May hadn't said anything about it!

And then poor Betsy-May began to cry again, because she was really very ashamed of herself, and she couldn't help thinking of John, who had wanted the penny for a ball.

"Oh, Nanny! The penny was John's!" she sobbed. "He dropped it and I found it. And I didn't give it him when I knew he was looking for it, because I wanted it for a lollipop. And now my lollipop is spoilt, and John hasn't got his penny and he can't buy his ball! And I'm very sorry and miserable!"

"I see," said Nanny, and she took Betsy-May on her knee,

52

looking very solemn. "Suppose Tubby-dog got lost and some-body else found him and kept him instead of giving him back to you," she said. "Wouldn't that be dreadful?"

"Don't let him be lost," said Betsy-May, big tears rolling down her fat cheeks. "Oh, Nanny, I want to give the penny back to John now – but I've spent it. I do feel so unhappy."

"What did you say John was going to buy with his penny?" asked Nanny. "A ball?"

"Yes," said Betsy-May.

"Now what can we do about it?" said Nanny. "Can you think of anything to put things right, Betsy-May? It would be so nice."

Betsy-May thought very hard. And then she wiped her eyes and got off Nanny's knee. She went to her toy-cup-board and hunted in it. She found what she was looking for – a big red ball!

"I'll give John my best red ball," she said. "Will that put things right, Nanny? Will it make John happy, and make me feel better too?"

"Yes, I think so," said Nanny. "It's a very good idea of yours, Betsy-May. Let's go and find John, shall we, and see what he says about it?"

So Betsy-May put on her hat for the third time that morn-ing, and she and Nanny and Tubby set off to go to John's house. He lived just round the corner.

"John is playing in the garden," said John's mother, when Nanny knocked at the door. "You can go and find him if you like." So they went into the garden, and there was John, playing with his tricycle, giving all his toy animals a ride.

"Hallo, Betsy-May!" he said.

"Hallo, John!" said Betsy-May. "I've come to tell you that I found your penny to-day, and I spent it on a red lollipop, and now I'm very sorry. So I've brought you my red ball, instead of your penny. Will you have it?"

"Oh, Betsy-May! What a beautiful ball!" said John in delight. He bounced it. "Can you really spare it?"

"No, I can't really," said Betsy-May. "But I'm giving it to you to put something right. I was sorry about your penny, you see. I would give it to you back, but I've spent it now. Do you think my ball will do instead?"

"It's *much* better than a penny, Betsy-May!" cried John. "Why, the ball I was going to buy was quite tiny. This is such a lovely big one. Oh, thank you. It *is* nice of you."

Betsy-May felt suddenly happy again. She badly wanted her ball, but she wanted everything to be right again even more.

"Well, it's your ball now," she said.

"Did you like the lollipop?" asked John.

"I didn't eat it," said Betsy-May. "It dropped on the floor. I expect my puppy has eaten it by now."

"Well, have one of my sweets," said John. He fetched a little bag and Betsy-May took a toffee.

"Thank you," she said. "I love toffees."

"Come along home now," said Nanny. "Tubby-dog is trampling on the flowers." So they went back home, and Betsy-May sucked her toffee and felt pleased.

"I shan't ever keep things that don't belong to me again,"

she told Nanny. "It made me feel horrid. Are you sure everything is right and happy again now, Nanny?"

"*Quite* sure," said Nanny. "You can nearly always put things right if you try hard enough, you know, Betsy-May. So just remember that!"

BETSY-MAY LENDS HER GOLLIWOG

Betsy-May had a great many toys, but best of all she loved her old golliwog. He had a red coat and blue trousers, and his black face always smiled. His hair was very thick and untidy, and no matter how much Betsy-May brushed it, it would never go right.

One day Betsy-May had a friend to tea. It was Peter, and she liked him very much. Sometimes she went to tea with him, and then they played with Peter's train. But when Peter came to tea with Betsy-May they always played with her dolls and animals.

This afternoon they had a lovely tea, with egg sandwiches, iced cakes and chocolate biscuits. Then they said their grace and got down to play. Peter found Betsy-May's golliwog, and he picked him up.

"I like this golliwog," he said. "He's smiling. Look, Betsy-May, what is he laughing at?"

"I don't know," said Betsy-May. "He's always laughing. Don't hold him too tightly, Peter. He doesn't like being squeezed too much."

Peter played with the golliwog all the time. Then he wanted to undress him.

"I don't undress him," said Betsy-May.

"But he wants to go to bed," said Peter.

"He doesn't," said Betsy-May.

"He does. He told me so," said Peter.

"Well, I didn't hear him," said Betsy-May. "And I know him a lot better than you do, Peter."

Peter began to undress him. The red coat was stitched up, so Peter had to pull the stitches undone. Then he undid the

56

blue trousers – and there was Golly in just his soft black body, with no clothes at all.

"He doesn't look nice," said Betsy-May. "He doesn't like it."

"He's smiling, so he does like it," said Peter. "I love your golliwog, Betsy-May. Where is his nightdress?"

"He hasn't got one," said Betsy-May. "I wish he had. I don't like him all black like that."

They tried on a doll's nightdress, but it was much too big. There was nothing to fit him at all.

Then it was time for Peter to go home with his Nanny. "Come along," said Nanny. "We must go. Bedtime, Peter."

"I want to take Betsy-May's golly home just for to-night," said Peter. "I'll bring him back to-morrow."

"Will you lend Peter your golly?" asked Betsy-May's Nanny. "He will take great care of him."

"I don't want Peter to have him," said Betsy-May, her face going very red. "He's cold. He hasn't got his clothes on."

"Well we'll put his clothes on," said Betsy-May's Nanny. "Then he will be all right."

But Golly's clothes could not be found. So he had to go without any, and Betsy-May was very unhappy. But she knew she must be kind to a visitor, so she didn't say what she felt. She kissed Peter and said good-bye. He clutched Golly and went out with him, very happy. He thought Golly was the nicest toy he had ever seen.

Betsy-May had her bath and went to bed. But when she was in bed she thought of her golliwog, all alone in a strange place, without any nightdress on to keep him warm, and she cried.

"What's the matter, Betsy-May?" asked her Nanny, surprised. "Have you got a pain?"

"No," said Betsy-May. "I'm thinking about poor Golly. I wish I hadn't let Peter have him. I wanted him myself."

"It was very kind of you to lend him to Peter," said Nanny tucking her up. "Don't worry about him. I expect Peter's Nanny will wrap him up in a shawl or something so that he will not be cold. Peter *was* so pleased to have him for a night. He will bring him back to-morrow."

Betsy-May went to sleep. She felt glad she had been kind to Peter, and she hoped he would be kind to Golly.

The next afternoon Betsy-May met Peter when he went out for his walk. And Peter had Golly with him!

"Betsy-May, I've brought your golliwog back," he said. "I cuddled him all night! He was very happy and so was I."

He held Golly out to Betsy-May, who stared at him in surprise.

"He's got a dress on," she said.

"Oh yes! Nanny said he ought to have a nighdress, so she made him one whilst I was eating my supper. Isn't it beautiful? But my Nanny says he really ought to have pyjamas, so she's going to make him those too, to-night. She thought you might like them for him, as you had been so kind and let me have your Golly," said Peter.

Betsy-May was so pleased that she couldn't say a word. She hugged her golliwog and beamed at everyone. Then she found her tongue.

"Oh, I've *always* wanted a nightie for Golly and I never had one that fitted him – and now he's got one, and he's going to have pyjamas too. Oh, I *am* happy!"

"What a good thing you were kind to Peter and lent him Golly!" said Nanny. "Kindness always comes back to you when you give it to others, Betsy-May!"

And now Betsy-May's golly is very grand. He goes to bed one night in a nightdress and the next night in pyjamas. Wouldn't you like to see him?

BETSY-MAY HAS A PARTY

Betsy-May was really very excited. She was going to a party at Peter's house the very next day! Nanny had finished making her a blue silk smock, and Mother had bought her a new blue ribbon for her golden hair.

And then, will you believe it, poor Betsy-May woke up with a sniffly nose on the very day of the party!

"Oh, Betsy-May, how disappointing! You can't go to the party with a cold," said Mother.

"Why not?" said Betsy-May. "I don't mind!"

"You might give your cold to the others," said Mother.

"Oh, I won't," said Betsy-May. "I'll keep it for myself, Mother, really I will."

But it was no use. Nobody can go to a party with a cold, so Betsy-May's blue smock had to be put away. Betsy-May cried and cried and cried.

"Now, now," said Nanny, "Cheer up. You are not very bad, so you can get up after dinner. And do dry your eyes, because I want you to give a party this afternoon."

Betsy-May was surprised. She dried her eyes and looked at Nanny.

"Who shall I give the party to?" she asked.

"To Golliwog and Teddy and Angela and the pink rabbit and the sailor doll, and the kitten as well," said Nanny.

"But I shall give them my cold if I have a party," said Betsy-May.

"They've all got colds," said Nanny. "So it will be all right. They will bring their handkerchiefs so that they can sneeze into them if they want to."

Well, Betsy-May felt quite excited after that. She got up after dinner, and dear me, Nanny put on her new blue smock and hair-ribbon, and a woolly coat in case she felt cold. So she felt just like a party, of course!

"Now you must get out your best tea-service whilst I get ready the cakes and things," said Nanny. "You will want six cups and saucers, and one saucer without a cup for the kitten. Put out the teapot, the sugar-basin and the milk-jug too."

Betsy-May was very busy. She got her little table and laid a white cloth on it. She put out the cups and saucers and plates. She set the big teapot, the sugar-basin and the milk-jug in the middle. It looked lovely.

"This is the chocolate cake," said Nanny, and she gave Betsy-May a large chocolate that was cut in thin slices all the way along! It looked just like a little chocolate cake! Betsy-May put it on the table.

"And here are the jellies," said Nanny, and she gave Betsy-May a dish of seven boiled sweets, pink and yellow and red and green. They looked just like jellies, except that they didn't shiver and shake.

"And here is some jammy bread," said Nanny, and she gave Betsy-May some little pieces of biscuit, with dabs of jam on them. She had cut the biscuit into tiny squares and it looked very like slices of bread and butter with jam.

"And this is a special marzipan cake," said Nanny, cutting a long marzipan sweet into slices. "I hope everyone will have some. Just go and ask the toys if they would rather have tea, milk, or lemonade to drink, Betsy-May."

Betsy-May went to ask them. She ran back to Nanny.

"They said they'd like lemonade," she said. Betsy-May liked lemonade too, so that was lucky. Nanny filled the teapot and the milk-jug with lemonade, and she put some tiny coffee sugars into the basin. Then Betsy-May dressed the toys in their best and went to look for the kitten.

"You are to come to my party," she said to the kitten, and

she brushed its fur with her doll's brush. When she carried the kitten to the nursery she saw that all the six toys had come to sit on their chairs round the table. And will you believe it, they all had tiny white handkerchiefs! Well, really! Betsy-May was so surprised.

"I've got my handerkerchief too," she said to the toys. "Now let's begin the party!"

Betsy-May poured out cups of lemonade for everyone. The teapot poured beautifully, and soon the little cups were full. Betsy-May drank them all, because that is the right thing to do at a dolls' tea-party. The kitten upset the milk-jug, but there was only a drop of lemonade left there, so it didn't matter.

Everyone took a jelly on his plate. Then they were offered slices of chocolate cake and marzipan cake. They had the bread and jam last of all. Everybody had some on his plate, but Betsy-May ate all the food. Toys are much too polite to eat very much.

Mother came in, in the middle of the party. She *was* pleased to see Betsy-May looking so happy.

"Why, nobody would think you had missed a lovely

treat!" she said. "You aren't making a bit of a fuss, Betsy-May. You are a good little girl."

"I'm giving a tea-party," said Betsy-May. "Can't you see my best blue smock on? Nanny, can I give Mother a cup of tea?"

So Nanny poured some more lemonade into the teapot, and Mother and Betsy-May solemnly had two cups each.

"Your cold is much better, Betsy-May," said Nanny.

"How funny!" said Betsy-May. "All my toys' colds are better too. They've *just* told me so!"

BETSY-MAY'S BEAUTIFUL BROOCH

Betsy-May had a beautiful brooch. It was shaped just like a white daisy, and it looked very real indeed. Betsy-May loved it. She wore it every time she went out to tea, and felt very proud of it.

One day Peter asked her to go to tea and play in the garden afterwards. Nanny couldn't take her, but Peter's Nanny said she would look after Betsy-May well, so Mother said she would take her to Peter's house and leave her there.

Betsy-May had on a pink frock, and a new pink jersey that Nanny had knitted for her. It had no collar at all, but just a little round neck, and Mother pulled the collar of the dress out so that it lay prettily on the jersey.

"There!" she said. "That looks nice. But just remember, Betsy-May, that when you go in to tea you must take off your jersey – and when you go out to play in the garden you must put it on again."

"I'll remember, Mother," said Betsy-May. "Can I have my daisy-brooch on? Nanny always lets me when I go out to tea."

"Yes," said Mother. She found the daisy brooch and pinned it on the front of Betsy-May's pink jersey. It looked very nice. Then Mother took Betsy-May's hand and they set off to Peter's house.

It was nearly tea-time when they got there, so Betsy-May went straight indoors. There was a lovely tea, with buttery buns, raspberry jam and animal biscuits.

"Now you may both get down and go and play in the garden for a little while," said Nanny. So they got down, washed their hands and put on their gum boots.

"I must remember to put on my jersey," said Betsy-May.

"And I must put on my coat," said Peter. "Do you know, Betsy-May, I can put my coat on all by myself, and do up the three buttons. Can you put your jersey on by yourself, or are you too little?"

Now Betsy-May had never put her jersey on by herself before, but, when Peter asked her that, she felt that she really must put it on without Nanny's help.

So she struggled into it somehow, and Peter pulled it down for her. Betsy-May felt quite proud. There was only a little button to do up and Peter managed to do that.

"We've put our coat and jersey on by ourselves!" called Peter to his Nanny, as they ran down the path.

"Clever children!" said Nanny, who was washing up the nursery tea-things. "You are a great help to me!"

Now, when Peter and Betsy-May had been playing at trains for a long time, Betsy-May felt tired. So she sat down on the seat, panting, and looked at Peter.

"Let's be people waiting for the train," she said. "I can't be the train any more. My legs won't run."

"All right," said Peter. "I'll show you my button. I picked it up in the road yesterday. I think it must be off a soldier's coat because it is bright and shiny."

He showed Betsy-May the button, and then Betsy-May remembered her daisy brooch.

"Oh, you must see my beautiful daisy brooch!" she said. "It's on the front of my jersey. Can you see it?"

Peter looked. "No," he said, "I can't see it. It isn't there."

"But it must be!" said Betsy-May, in alarm. "My Mummy pinned it there this afternoon."

She pulled her jersey out and looked up and down it. But Peter was right. The daisy brooch was not there.

"I must have dropped it, Peter," said Betsy-May, most upset. "Oh, I must look for it. It was a most beautiful brooch."

So they began to look for it. They hunted everywhere that they had played trains – but although there were hundreds of white daisies growing in the grass there was no white daisy brooch to be found.

Betsy-May began to cry. "I did so love my daisy brooch," she sobbed. Nanny came running out to see what was the matter.

"Oh, we shall soon find it!" she said, when Peter had told her about the brooch. "I'll help you to look."

But not even Nanny could find it, although she had very sharp eyes indeed. So it seemed as if Betsy-May must go on being sad and unhappy, and neither Peter nor she would enjoy their play any more.

And then Peter found the brooch. Well, really, you would never, never guess where it was!

"Betsy-May, Betsy-May, your brooch is on your back!" suddenly shouted Peter. "It's pinned at the back of you. It's on your jersey, quite safe!"

"But my Mother pinned it at the front, just here," said Betsy-May, puzzled. "How could it get round to the back?"

"Oh, Betsy-May, I know what happened!" cried Nanny. "You put your jersey on by yourself – and you put it on back to front, you little goose! So, of course, the brooch is now at the back instead of at the front. No wonder we couldn't see it pinned on your front, when all the time it was on your back!"

Well, would you believe it! Nanny unpinned the brooch and put it on the front again, because it didn't matter which way Betsy-May wore the jersey. So she was happy once more and played for a long time with Peter. And how Mother and Nanny laughed when they heard the joke!

BETSY-MAY GOES TO DANCING

Every Wednesday afternoon Betsy-May went to a dancing-class. Nanny dressed her up in a pretty frock, tied one of her best ribbons on her hair, and put her in the little pram to wheel her to the school.

Betsy-May always wanted to walk, because she thought it looked babyish going to her dancing class in the pram. But Nanny said no, she must ride, or she would be tired before she got there.

There were nine children in Betsy-May's class. Betsy-May knew them all, and she used to say their names to herself when she was in bed.

"Alice, Jane, Gillian, Rosemary, Nicky, Kenneth, John, me . . . and Susan."

Betsy-May always put Susan last of all, because she didn't like her. Susan was big. Susan was clever. Susan had learnt dancing before, and she could do everything much better than Betsy-May.

"I wish Susan couldn't do everything," Betsy-May said to Nanny.

"Soon you will be like Susan, and will be able to do everything too," said Nanny. "This is only your first term, Betsy-May."

One Wednesday everyone was told to bring skipping-ropes to the next class. Betsy-May hadn't a skipping-rope. It was great fun to go and buy one at the toy-shop. Betsy-May chose one with red handles and a tiny bell on each handle that rang loudly. She thought it was the loveliest skipping-rope in the world.

But oh dear, Betsy-May couldn't skip with it at all! She tried and tried at the next dancing-class, but the rope seemed to tie itself round her feet in a very queer way. Poor Betsy-May spent all her time lifting her feet out of the tangled rope.

Susan skipped most beautifully. Up and down, up and down on her toes she went, swinging her rope over her head and under her jumping feet. It was wonderful.

"You *are* a baby not to be able to skip!" said Susan, teasing Betsy-May.

Betsy-May was sure that everyone in the class must have heard what Susan said. She went very red and the tears came into her eyes.

"You are a very horrid girl, Susan," Betsy-May said, in such a loud voice that everybody was startled and looked round at her. Betsy-May ran to Nanny and pulled at her.

"I want to go home," she said. "I don't like dancing any more. I want to go home."

The class was nearly over, so Nanny took Betsy-May home, very much puzzled. "Why did you tell Susan she was a horrid girl?" she asked. "That was unkind."

"Susan said I was a baby because I couldn't skip," said Betsy-May. "I don't want to go to dancing any more. I don't like it. It isn't nice to be a baby, and I simply *can't* skip, Nanny."

"You will soon learn, Betsy-May," said Nanny. But dear me, when next Wednesday came, Betsy-May would *not* go to her dancing class. She even screamed and kicked when Nanny tried to dress her, and that was a thing she hardly ever did.

So Nanny didn't take her. Betsy-May was glad. Now Susan wouldn't see she was a baby and couldn't skip.

The next afternoon Nanny went a different way for a walk with Betsy-May – and they met Susan walking out with *her* Nanny, and her baby brother in a pram.

"You didn't come to the dancing-class, Betsy-May," said Susan. "Did you have a cold?"

"No," said Betsy-May, going red. She hoped that Nanny wouldn't tell why she hadn't gone.

"We had skipping again," said Susan. "And I skipped the best."

"Well, this is your third term at dancing," said her Nanny. "I would be ashamed of you if you didn't skip the best. You should be helping the little ones, now that you skip so well."

"Oh," said Susan.

"That's a splendid idea!" said Betsy-May's Nanny. "I wonder if you would like to come to tea with us to-morrow,

Susan, if Nanny will let you, and bring your skipping-rope, and help Betsy-May to skip? She is so quick that she would soon learn."

"Oh, I'd *love* to do that," said Susan; "can I, Nanny?"

"Of course," said her Nanny. So the next day Susan came to tea, and brought her skipping-rope. After they had had a lovely tea they went into the garden with their ropes. Betsy-May was afraid that Susan would still think she was a baby – but Susan was very nice.

She was proud to teach Betsy-May. She showed her how to jump with her feet close together. Then she showed her how to swing the rope over her head and under her feet.

Betsy-May tried and tried – and then, quite suddenly, she could do it! The rope swung under her jumping feet, and she was skipping!

"Nanny, Nanny! I can skip!" she shouted. Susan was just as pleased as Betsy-May.

"Betsy-May is clever," she told Nanny. And Betsy-May felt very big and old. She loved Susan. She thought she was wonderful because she had been kind and had taught Betsy-May how to skip. Susan loved Betsy-May too, because she was proud of her.

And the next Wednesday Betsy-May said: "I am longing to go to dancing, Nanny! Please hurry up and dress me! I can skip now. And Susan will be there. She's the best girl of all!"

Nanny smiled a little smile to herself, and dressed Betsy-May for dancing. Goodness me, you should have seen how well she skipped that afternoon, and how Susan smiled at her. The dancing-mistress was *most* surprised!

BETSY-MAY AND THE GARDENER

Betsy-May loved the gardener. He came on Wednesdays and Fridays, and made the flowers grow nicely. Betsy-May always loved Wednesdays and Fridays because then she could go and talk to Biddle the gardener.

"Biddle is a lovely name," she said to Nanny. "I wish I was called Biddle."

"Well, you can call your new sailor doll Biddle," said Nanny. "He hasn't got a name yet."

"No. I'll wait till I have a gardener doll, and then *he* shall be called Biddle," said Betsy-May. "It would be a pity to waste it on Sailor Doll."

One day Biddle the gardener gave Betsy-May a bunch of snowdrops that he had picked for her from his own garden at home. Betsy-May was so suprised and pleased that she went quite pink. She remembered to say "Thank you very much, Biddle," and then she rushed indoors to show Nanny and Mummy.

"Well, how *kind* of Biddle!" said Mummy. "He must like you very much to give you such pretty flowers, Betsy-May."

"I shall put them in my own little vase and have them in the middle of the nursery table," said Betsy-May. So she got her vase, filled it carefully with water from the tap, and arranged her snowdrops one by one. There were such a lot. Betsy-May thought their little white heads were like bells. But they didn't ring. She shook each one to see.

The next thing that Biddle did was to give Betsy-May two cigarette cards. They had animals on, and Betsy-May thought

72

they were really lovely. There was an elephant on one and a bear on the other.

"Oh thank you, Biddle, thank you very much," said Betsy-May, proudly. "Do you know, Peter has cigarette

cards too? He's the boy that comes to tea with me sometimes. He has shown me his cards – but I don't think he's got an elephant *or* a bear. I didn't think I would ever have any cigarette cards, but now I have."

Betsy-May looked at her cigarette cards about a hundred times a day. She showed them to Peter when she met him one afternoon and Peter wanted them.

"I'm afraid they're quite mine," said Betsy-May, firmly. "Biddle gave them to me. He wouldn't like me to give them to anybody."

"I'll give you two other cards if you'll give me the elephant and bear ones," said Peter.

But Betsy-May simply wouldn't hear of it. She felt prouder than ever of the cards now that she knew even

Peter wanted them. She ran round Biddle like a little dog whenever he came, and they talked about all kinds of things together.

And then Biddle gave Betsy-May a curious stone he had dug up in the garden. It was blue, with pink lines running round it. Betsy-May felt sure it was magic.

"You can have it, Miss," said Biddle. He always called Betsy-May Miss and it made her feel grown-up. Betsy-May stared at the stone and longed to have it. But she felt it was really too precious for Biddle to give away.

"No," she said. "It's yours, Biddle. You found it. You can keep it and show it to me sometimes."

But Biddle only laughed, took her little pink hand, pressed the blue stone into it, and shut her fingers over it. "Now it's yours!" he said.

Well, Betsy-May was so pleased with this stone that she wondered and wondered what she could do for Biddle. So she asked him when his birthday was.

"It's next Wednesday," said Biddle.

"Really?" said Betsy-May, pleased. "Then I shall buy you a present, Biddle, because you are really so very kind to me."

Betsy-May went to her money-box. She asked Nanny to empty it and see if there was enough to buy Biddle a present. But there was only twopence inside.

"Well, I can buy something nice for two pennies, can't I?" said Betsy-May. "Let's go to the toy-shop this afternoon, Nanny."

So they went. Nanny thought Biddle would like a nice gold stud for twopence, but Betsy-May said no. Then Nanny said that a note-book and pencil would be useful, but still Betsy-May shook her head.

Suddenly she saw a little tiny bell. She picked it up. It rang! Betsy-May remembered the snowdrops that didn't

74

ring their bells, and she said: "Nanny! This is the noise that snowdrops would make if they could ring their white bells."

She shook the little bell. It made a beautiful little tinkle, as sweet as could be. "I shall buy this for Biddle," said Betsy-May. "He would love it."

But Nanny was quite cross. "It is silly to buy a bell for Biddle," she said. "He would *much* rather have a note-book and pencil, Betsy-May."

"Nanny, I know Biddle would love this better than anything in the shop," said Betsy-May. "Please, I do want it."

So Nanny let her buy it and Betsy-May walked home in great excitement with the bell wrapped up in paper. And do you know, she could hear it tinkling through the paper! It was most exciting.

Betsy-May had to wait till the next Wednesday to give it to Biddle. She grew so fond of the little tinkling bell that she really thought she would like to keep it herself. But she had bought it for Biddle, so she knew she couldn't.

Wednesday came, and so did Biddle. Betsy-May rushed out to him in the garden. "Many happy returns of the day, Biddle!" she cried. "I've got a present for you! Look!"

She gave him the bell. He took it and looked at it. Then he rang it.

"Well, if that isn't the nicest little bell I've ever seen in my life!" he said. "Thank you, Miss."

"Is it the nicest present you've had?" asked Betsy-May, jumping round happily.

"The very nicest," said Biddle. "And do you know what I'm going to do with it, Miss? I'm going to take this bit of string, look – and thread it through the tiny handle of the bell – see? And tie the bell to my waistcoat button like this – and then when I walk or work my bell will ring – and you'll know exactly where I am in the garden!"

He took a few steps and the bell tinkled. Betsy-May squealed with delight. "Now I shall always know where you are!" she cried. "Oh, Biddle, isn't it a good idea?"

So now Biddles tinkles wherever he goes, and Betsy-May *always* knows exactly where he is!

BETSY-MAY AND THE SCARECROW

Once when Betsy-May went for a walk with Nanny across the fields, they came to a big stile.

"We'll go over the stile," said Nanny. "It will take us a short way home."

So Nanny climbed over the stile and Betsy-May climbed through it. But when she looked round the big field they were going to cross, Betsy-May saw a scarecrow standing there, and she didn't like him at all.

"What's that?" she said, and she pointed to the scarecrow.

"That's a funny man the farmer has made out of sticks and old clothes," said Nanny. "He is kind because he stands out here in the field all day and scares away the birds from the farmer's corn."

"He scares me too," said Betsy-May. "I don't like him. I don't want to go home this way."

"He won't hurt you," said Nanny. "He is a great help to the farmer. He only has one wooden leg, look – he has to stand still all day long and never goes for a walk. It must be lonely for him. Shall we call out: 'Hallo, scarecrow! How do you do?' He won't feel so lonely then."

"No, I don't want to talk to him at all," said Betsy-May. "He looks horrid to me. His arms stick out so straight."

The scarecrow stood still in the middle of the field, and seemed to look at Betsy-May and Nanny. He had a turnip for a head, and on it was a broken old hat of the farmer's. He wore a ragged old coat too, with dragged-down pockets. He had a pair of trousers on his one leg, and a dirty scarf round his neck.

"I don't want to go home this way," said Betsy-May, and she dragged at Nanny's hand. "I want to go home the other way."

"Very well," said Nanny. "But I do think you might have just said 'Hallo!' to the scarecrow."

"I don't want to," said Betsy-May. "He might say something back to me."

They went back home the long way and Betsy-May was very tired. She didn't say any more about the scarecrow, and neither did Nanny. But the next week they had to go that way again, and Betsy-May saw him once more.

"Why, there's the dear old scarecrow!" said Nanny, cheerfully. "How nice to see him again!"

"*I* don't think he's nice," said Betsy-May. "I still don't like him. I think he's horrid to frighten the birds."

"Well, the farmer can't have the birds eating up his corn, can he?" said Nanny. "We get our bread from the corn, you know. If the scarecrow didn't frighen away the birds, they would eat the corn, and then we wouldn't have our nice brown bread for tea."

"I think the scarecrow is horrid," said Betsy-May, "and I won't go by him. Let's go home the other way."

So once more they went home the long way. And the next morning Betsy-May told Biddle the gardener about the scarecrow. Biddle always wore the little bell that Betsy-May had given him, and he made a tinkling noise whenever he moved.

He listened when Betsy-May told him about the scarecrow. "You know, Biddle, he's a very nasty person," said Betsy-May. "He scares the birds, and he's got a turnip head that looks horrid. I wish the farmer would take him away."

Biddle leaned on his spade and looked down at Betsy-May. "I can tell you something about that scarecrow," he said. "But you won't tell anybody else, will you?"

"Is it a secret then?" asked Betsy-May, excited.

"It's *his* secret," said Biddle.

"The scarecrow's secret, do you mean?" asked Betsy-May, puzzled.

"Yes," said Biddle. "And a mighty fine secret it is too. I pass by him every day when I go to work, Miss, and I always say 'Good morning, scarecrow!' to the old fellow. And maybe that's why I got to know his secret."

"I want to know it too," said Betsy-May.

"Well, you'll have to go close up to him, and look in his pocket, if you want to know his secret," said Biddle. "Ah, it's a big secret. It's a wonderful secret too. But you have to go close to him and look."

"I don't think I'd like to do that," said Betsy-May. "He scares the birds and he might scare me too."

"Well, now I'll tell you something else," said Biddle. "That old scarecrow, he *likes* birds!"

"How do you know?" asked Betsy-May.

"Ah! You go and look in his pocket and you'll soon see I'm telling you the truth!" said Biddle. "But don't you tell anybody. It's his secret, and mine – and now it'll be yours if you go and look."

Well, Betsy-May thought and thought about it, and the more she thought about it, the more she wanted to find out the secret. So that afternoon she asked Nanny to go the walk that took them to the scarecrow's field.

Nanny was surprised. "You don't like that walk," she said. "It's such a long way home again."

"But we can go the short way, through the farmer's field," said Betsy-May.

"But you won't go by the poor old scarecrow," said Nanny, still puzzled.

"I might to-day," said Betsy-May. "Biddle says the scarecrow has a secret to tell me. Please let's go, Nanny."

"Well, of course we will," said Nanny, pleased. So they went that way.

Betsy-May saw the scarecrow standing just as he always stood, his turnip-head a little on one side. She thought he looked nicer. After all, he must be quite kind if Biddle liked him.

"You stay here, Nanny," she said. "I want to go alone to the scarecrow."

Nanny was astonished. Why, Betsy-May had been too scared of the scarecrow even to go through his field – and now here she was, wanting to go right up to him alone!

"Very well," she said. "I'll stay just here." So she stayed, and Betsy-May ran up to the old scarecrow. "Hallo," she said softly. But he didn't answer. She looked in one of his coat-pockets – and whatever *do* you think she saw? Guess!

She saw a robin's nest there, with a little robin sitting on her eggs! She didn't fly off when she saw Betsy-May. She sat and looked at her. Betsy-May was so delighted that she made a little squeal of joy.

"So *that's* your secret, dear old scarecrow!" she said. "Oh, now I know you don't really scare the birds. You love them! And you don't scare me any more either. I couldn't be scared of anybody who had a robin's nest in his pocket! Goodbye, dear old scarecrow. I'll come and see you often now!"

She ran back to Nanny. "The scarecrow has shown me his secret, and I love him now," said Betsy-May. "I want to go this walk every single day, Nanny!"

"Good gracious me!" said Nanny. "You *have* given me a nice surprise!"

BETSY-MAY AND TINKER-DOG

One day Nanny took Betsy-May to call on Mrs. Harrison, who often did some sewing for Mummy. Mrs. Harrison lived in a tiny white cottage with a big garden at the back, and she had a little dog called Tinker.

Mrs. Harrison opened the door and asked them in. It was rather an exciting house because you walked straight into the kitchen from the front door. There wasn't any hall at all.

"Where's the hall gone?" asked Betsy-May, looking round.

"There never was a hall," said Mrs. Harrison, laughing.

"Oh. I wish I lived in a house like this," said Betsy-May. "I wish our kitchen was just inside the front door. Where's Tinker, Mrs. Harrison?"

"Tinker-dog is in the garden," said Mrs. Harrison. "I'll call him."

Tinker-dog came rushing in, and licked Betsy-May's hand. Then he licked Nanny's hand.

"Lie down, Tinker-dog," said Mrs. Harrison. Then she turned to Nanny.

"If you could wait just for ten minutes, I could finish putting on the hooks of this dress," she said. "Then you could take it back with you."

"Very well," said Nanny, and she sat down in a rocking-chair. Betsy-May thought it was a lovely chair, and she hoped Nanny would let her have a turn at rocking soon.

"Would the little girl like a cake?" asked Mrs. Harrison, going to a cupboard. "I've got some little rock-buns here that I made myself."

"Well," said Nanny, "if she'll eat her dinner up nicely . . ."

"Oh, I will, I will," said Betsy-May, pleased. So Mrs. Harrison gave her a little rock-bun. Betsy-May took a bite. It was most delicious. She held the bun in her hand and chewed the bit in her mouth – and then she suddenly felt something touching her hand. She looked down.

It was Tinker-dog. And he was eating her bun! Yes, there he sat close beside Betsy-May nibbling at her rock-bun! And, before Betsy-May could draw her hand away, Tinker-dog got the whole of the bun and swallowed it down.

Betsy-May didn't know what to do. She didn't like to tell tales to Mrs. Harrison about her own dog. She wiped her fingers down her coat and Nanny saw her.

"Good gracious, child! Have you eaten the bun already?" she said. "That was much too quick! How naughty of you!"

"I didn't," said Betsy-May. "This horrid greedy dog ate it. He licked it out of my hand."

"You bad dog, Tinker," cried Mrs. Harrison, and she smacked Tinker-dog hard. He yelped. Betsy-May felt sorry for him, but she didn't like him at all.

"Well, I'm afraid all the other buns are made of ginger," said Mrs. Harrison, looking into her tin. "You won't like those, Betsy-May. But wait a minute. I believe I've got one last chocolate in this chocolate box!"

She opened the box, and sure enough there was a nice round chocolate there. Mrs. Harrison gave it to Betsy-May.

"Thank you, Mrs. Harrison," said Betsy-May. She was just going to pop it into her mouth when somehow or other she dropped it on to the floor.

And do you know, before she could pick it up, Tinker-dog pounced on it and gobbled it down without even biting it!

Betsy-May stared at Tinker-dog in anger. "You had my cake and now you've got my chocolate," she said. "I think you are the worst dog in the world."

Mrs. Harrison smacked Tinker-dog again and turned him out of the room into the garden. But there were no more chocolates and Betsy-May felt very sad.

"Well, it was your own fault, Betsy-May," said Nanny. "You should learn not to drop things. Mrs. Harrison, the room is a bit hot for Betsy-May – would you mind if she took her ball into the garden for a little while?"

"Certainly," said Mrs. Harrison. "Trot along out, Betsy-May."

So Betsy-May went out, very pleased. But in the garden was Tinker-dog, and he came rushing up to her.

"Go away," said Betsy-May, and she pushed him. "I don't like rushing dogs. And I think you are very unkind and greedy and naughty. You are a BAD DOG!"

Tinker-dog dropped his long tail and looked sad. But Betsy-May would not forgive him.

"You ate my bun," she said. "And you ate my chocolate. I don't like you any more. I don't like dogs at all now. You are a BAD DOG."

Tinker-dog went to a corner and lay down there, looking very miserable. He looked sadly at Betsy-May with his big brown eyes. She bounced her ball. Tinker-dog wagged his tail a little. He loved balls.

"No," said Betsy-May, sternly. "You shan't play with my ball. I shall tell Mrs. Harrison if you try to get it. You are a very horrid little dog."

Tinker-dog put his head on his paws and sighed. He was very unhappy. But Betsy-May still didn't like him. She bounced her ball and called Tinker-dog names.

"Horrid dog! Nasty dog! Greedy dog!" she kept saying. Then she began to throw her ball into the air to show Tinker-dog how well she could catch it. It went very high and very far, and fell among some bushes. Betsy-May ran to find it. But she couldn't. She hunted simply everywhere for it, but her ball was gone.

"Oh dear!" said Betsy-May. "It's my best one, my nice red one. Oh, *where* can it be?"

Then Tinker-dog came out from his corner and ran to the bushes. He dived into the middle of one and what do you think? He found the ball and brought it to Betsy-May! He laid it down by her feet, looked up at her and wagged his tail.

"Woof!" he said joyfully.

"Oh, you *kind* dog!" said Betsy-May. "After all the horrid things I've said to you! You've found my ball! Nanny, listen! Nanny! Tinker-dog found my ball after I'd been very, very angry with him."

"Well," said Nanny, coming to fetch her, "you know

Tinker-dog didn't *mean* to steal your cake and your chocolate, Betsy-May. He thought you were holding it out for him to nibble, and he thought you had really thrown down your chocolate for him to eat. Dogs don't understand as children do. You should forgive him and try to understand."

"Oh I do, I do!" cried Betsy-May and she patted Tinker-dog. "I'll bring you a bone tomorrow, Tinker, because you found my ball for me. And I *do* like dogs, so don't think I mean what I said, will you?"

"Woof, woof!" said Tinker, rushing round happily. So I expect he understood, don't you?

BETSY-MAY IS SHY

Once, when Betsy-May went out with Mummy, they met some of Mummy's friends.

They all looked at Betsy-May and they nodded and smiled at her.

"What a dear little girl!" said one.

"And do you go to school yet, dear?" said another. Betsy-May didn't answer. She felt shy when so many people looked at her all at once.

Mummy was cross. "Betsy-May, shake hands and speak nicely," she said.

One of the ladies held out her hand to Betsy-May, and said: "How-do-you-do, Betsy-May?"

But Betsy-May turned her back and wouldn't shake hands or speak. Mummy was quite ashamed of her. When she got home she spoke to Nanny about Betsy-May's manners.

"We shall really have to teach her how to shake hands and say 'how-do-you-do' and 'quite-well-thank-you'," said Mummy.

But do you know, Betsy-May wouldn't learn! She put her hand behind her back when Mummy wanted to show her what to do. "I don't want to learn manners," she said. "I don't want to say 'how-do-you-do'. It's silly."

"I think she's a bit tired," said Nanny. "We will teach her another day, shall we, Mummy?"

So nobody said any more to Betsy-May about manners that day. But the next day Nanny spoke to Betsy-May and said: "Betsy-May, have you taught your toys their manners? Do they know how to shake hands and say how-do-you-do and quite-well-thank-you, and thank-you-for-having-me, after a party?"

"Of course they don't know," said Betsy-May.

"Well, I wish you would teach them," said Nanny. "Then at any rate I should know that the toys in my nursery knew their manners even if you didn't."

"I don't know how to teach them," said Betsy-May.

"Let me teach Teddy-Bear," said Nanny. "He looks as if he would love to learn. Now, Teddy, stand up. That's right. Put out your right hand – no, your *right* hand, Teddy – and shake my hand. Good boy! Now I'm going to say 'How-do-you-do' and you must say 'Quite well, thank you'!"

Nanny said: "How-do-you-do?" in a very polite voice, and then she pressed Teddy hard in the middle and he growled quickly four times and it sounded exactly like "quite well, thank you". Betsy-May thought he was very clever.

"Well," said Nanny, still talking to the bear. "You are learning very well indeed. But I have my work to do, so I'm afraid I can't teach you any more this morning. I'll give you another lesson to-morrow."

She went out of the room. Betsy-May stood and looked at her toys. She picked up Teddy and squeaked him again to make him say "quite well, thank you". He did sound clever.

Betsy-May arranged her three dolls, her teddy bear, her golliwog and the pink rabbit in a ring round her. Then she spoke to them.

"Toys, I'm going to teach you manners. My Mummy says everybody should learn manners. You must learn thank you and please, and how-do-you-do? and quite-well-thank-you, and thank-you-for-having-me, and I'm sorry, when you do anything wrong. Now please listen."

The toys sat and listened. The golliwog fell over and had

to be sat up again. Betsy-May squeaked them all to make them say "Thank you" and "Please".

Then she held out her hand to each one of them and said: "How do-you-do?" She didn't squeak them to make them answer. She pretended to answer herself and she spoke first of all in a teddy-bear voice, deep and growly.

"Quite well, thank you," she said. Then she shook hands with the sailor doll and said: "How-do-you-do, Sailor Doll?"

And she answered for the sailor doll in a jolly sort of voice: "Quite well, thank you!" Then she shook hands with the baby doll's little fat fingers, and said: "How do-you-do, Baby Doll?"

And she answered for the baby doll in a tiny high baby voice: "Quite well, thank you!"

It *was* fun teaching her toys manners. They were all very good indeed, except the golliwog, who kept falling over. Betsy-May showed each of them which his right hand was.

And then suddenly the door opened and in came Mummy with a friend. It was Mrs. White and she stood smiling at the door.

"Hallo, Betsy-May," said Mummy. "What are you doing?"

"I'm teaching my toys their manners," said Betsy-May. "Look, Mummy – watch Teddy Bear shaking hands with me and saying 'Quite well, thank you'!"

Mummy and Mrs. White watched. Teddy behaved beautifully. He shook hands, and then Betsy-May pressed him in the middle and he growled: "Quite well, thank you!"

"Well, your toys *have* got nice manners!" said Mrs. White.

"They are cleverer than Betsy-May! Fancy that!" said Mummy. "She hasn't learnt to shake hands and say 'Quite well, thank you' yet – but all her toys know how to."

"I know too," said Betsy-May at once. "I taught my toys, so of course I know. I've got nice manners too."

"I'm afraid you haven't, darling," said Mummy.

"Well, you say 'How-do-you-do?' to me, Mummy, and just see," said Betsy-May.

So Mummy pretended to be a lady and she walked forward, smiling, and holding out her hand. "How-do-you-do, Betsy-May?" she asked.

Betsy-May held out her right hand and walked to meet Mummy. "Quite well, thank you," she answered, in a very polite voice.

Then Mrs. White came forward too, holding out her hand, and saying "How-do-you-do, Betsy-May?" But Betsy-May wasn't at all shy now, and she held out her right hand to Mrs. White and answered: "Quite well, thank you!" most beautifully.

"Well, I *am* pleased with you!" said Mummy, and she smiled all over her face. "It *is* nice to have a little girl with such good manners!"

"Yes," said Betsy-May, "I know how you feel, Mummy. I feel just the same about my toys. I'm proud that they've got nice manners too. They will never be shy, I know – and neither will I!"

And Nanny *was* surprised that afternoon when they met Peter's Nanny out for a walk – because Betsy-May held out her right hand most politely and said: "How-do-you-do, Peter's Nanny?" Just like that!

BETSY-MAY AND THE SAILOR DOLL

One morning Betsy-May was very slow over her breakfast. Nanny got quite tired of waiting for her to eat her porridge.

"Do try and find the little man on your plate, under your porridge," said Nanny. "He's tired of being under the milk."

"He says he *likes* being under the milk," said Betsy-May, and she stirred her porridge so hard that it went out of her plate and spilt on the clean table-cloth.

"I think you must have got out of bed on the wrong side this morning," said Nanny, not at all pleased.

"It was the same side as usual," said Betsy-May, remembering. "I can't get out the other side, Nanny, because the wall is there."

Betsy-May was naughty after breakfast too. She found a pencil, and scribbled over the wall with it. Nanny really was cross then.

"Betsy-May, you know that you are not allowed a pencil till you are a big girl," she said.

"Well, you told me I was a very big girl yesterday when I didn't cry over my hurt knee," said Betsy-May. "Have I gone little again?"

"I think you must have," said Nanny, trying to wipe off the scribbles with a wet cloth. "It's a great pity."

"I want to play with my paint-box this morning," said Betsy-May, seeing it at the top of the toy cupboard.

"Not to-day," said Nanny. "You would only spill the water, and make a great mess. You are not big enough to-day to paint."

"I *am*!" shouted Betsy-May, and she stood herself in front of Nanny. "Look at me! Look at me! I nearly reach the ceiling! I want my paint-box."

"I never give things to little girls who shout," said Nanny, and she looked very solemn. Betsy-May hated Nanny to look solemn. She wondered if she should cry. She wondered if she should stamp.

But she didn't do either of those things. She did something else. She went to her toy cupboard, and snatched out some of her toys. First it was her wooden train. She threw it up into the air. Crash! It came down on the floor.

Then she snatched out a book and flung it over her head. Crash! It fell on the table.

She pulled out a little trumpet and flung it over the nursery. It nearly went into the fire. Nanny tried to shut the toy cupboard door, but before she could do it Betsy-May took out one more toy to throw.

It was her sailor doll. He wore a sailor suit, with a sailor hat on, and he was always smiling. Betsy-May loved him because of his smile. But she didn't think of that any more. She took hold of him and threw him high into the air. She heard a soft thud as he came down somewhere.

"Poor little Sailor," said Nanny, in a sad voice. "He thought you loved him – but just because you felt cross you threw him away. Poor little Sailor."

Suddenly Betsy-May felt dreadful. How *could* she have thrown her Sailor away? What did he think? Suppose he had broken his smile?

She looked round the nursery to find him. He wasn't on the floor. He wasn't on the table. He didn't seem to be anywhere!

"Where is Sailor Doll, Nanny?" she asked.

"Well, where did he go when you threw him?" said Nanny. "I didn't see, I was picking up the trumpet."

"I don't *know* where I threw him," said Betsy-May, very

much upset. "Oh, do find him for me, Nanny. I'm sorry I was so silly."

So Nanny helped Betsy-May to look for Sailor Doll. But they really couldn't seem to find him anywhere at all.

They looked under the table and the chairs. They looked behind the book-case. They looked behind the big wooden horse. But it wasn't any good. Sailor Doll had gone.

"Nanny, do you suppose – do you suppose he went into the *fire*?" asked Betsy-May, with tears in her eyes.

"Oh no, I shouldn't think so," said Nanny. "Never mind him now, Betsy-May – I expect he'll turn up sometime or other."

So Betsy-May got out her bricks and began to build a little house for Sailor Doll when he came back. She felt very sad to think that her bad temper should have made him disappear like that. Nanny was puzzled too. She couldn't *think* where he had gone!

"I'm just going downstairs for a few minutes to take in the dry clothes," Nanny said to Betsy-May. "I'll take the waste-paper basket down with me and empty it. I shan't be a minute."

Betsy-May went on building her house. She made a door and a window, so that Sailor Doll could walk in and out, and look out of the window whenever he liked. She took a tiny chair and put that in the house too.

Suddenly Nanny came back again – and what do you think she had in her hand? She had Sailor Doll!

"Look!" she said. "Here is dear old Sailor again!"

"Oh, *Nanny*! Where did you find him?" asked Betsy-May, with a squeal of joy. She ran to get him.

"You had thrown him into the waste-paper basket," said Nanny. "He had got all mixed up with the grape-fruit skin, and bits of paper and banana peel. Poor Sailor! And I emptied him right into the dustbin, Betsy-May!"

"Oh, *poor* Sailor Doll!" said Betsy-May. She smelt him. "He smells a bit of banana peel, Nanny. Oh, Nanny, suppose you hadn't seen him – you would have put the dustbin lid on him – and the dustman would have taken him away this afternoon!"

"So he would," said Nanny. "What a narrow escape he has had, Betsy-May! I do so hope you will not get into a bad temper again. You see, you make things so horrid for other people – why, just think what has happened to poor Sailor, who has always been as good as gold. You threw him into the waste-paper basket, and I put him into the dustbin! All because you were feeling rather naughty to-day."

Betsy-May listened. She nodded her head. "It was horrid of me," she said. "I don't think I shall do that again, because I don't want to make things horrid for Sailor or anybody. But oh look, Nanny – his smile is just a bit broken! This side, look! He is happy with one side of his mouth, but he is sad with the other."

"I expect that's what he feels like," said Nanny. "Well, never mind. He'll soon forget. But *you* mustn't forget. When you feel cross, just look at Sailor Doll's broken smile, and then you will stop yourself, and be your own happy self again. I wouldn't like you to break *my* smile like Sailor's, you know!" And Nanny smiled all over her face.

"I *couldn't* break your smile, Nanny!" said Betsy-May and she gave her a great big hug.

BETSY-MAY AT NIGHT

Sometimes Betsy-May was very naughty at night, after she had been put to bed. If she didn't go to sleep at once she would slip out of bed and dance round the bedroom!

If Mummy or Nanny heard her they would come up at once, very cross. Then Betsy-May would hop into bed and snuggle down, and pretend to be asleep. But they always knew she wasn't, and scolded her very hard.

"You will be so tired to-morrow that you will not be able to eat your breakfast," said Nanny.

"You will be too sleepy to go to your dancing class," said Mummy.

But the next day came, and Betsy-May always did eat her breakfast, and never was too tired to go to dancing, so she thought Mummy and Nanny must be wrong.

One night she got out of bed and went to the door. She wondered if there was anyone in the day-nursery. If Nanny was downstairs then Betsy-May could go in and finish the jigsaw puzzle she had begun doing before bedtime. She knew it was quite easy to finish and she did so badly want to.

So she crept across the passage and peeped in at the nursery door. Nobody was there at all. Her puzzle was still on the little table where she had left it. There were five pieces still to put in. It was an easy puzzle, one that Betsy-May loved because when it was done it was a rabbit eating a red carrot. She finished it and went back to bed happy.

But Nanny was most surprised to find the puzzle finished the next morning. She looked at Betsy-May and Betsy-May went rather pink and looked back at her.

"So you got out of bed last night and came into the day-nursery to finish your puzzle," said Nanny. "How very naughty, Betsy-May! One day you will be very sorry that your are so disobedient at night. Now in future I shall sit in the day-nursery till you are fast asleep."

Betsy-May was cross when Nanny said that. It was fun to get out of bed at night. It was exciting to creep about in the half-dark. But it wasn't any use the next few nights, because Nanny sat in the day-nursery with the door open, and could hear every sound that Betsy-May made.

Then one day Betsy-May had an invitation to Peter's birthday party. He would soon be seven, and he was going to have a fine party, with a birthday cake and seven candles on it.

Betsy-May was pleased. She loved parties. She planned to give Peter a little red wooden train she had seen in the toy-shop. He would like that.

"It's a good thing you have given up getting out of bed at night," said Nanny, "or you might make yourself too tired to go to Peter's party."

Now the night before the party Betsy-May was really too excited to go to sleep. She lay in her bed and tossed and turned, and thought about birthday cakes and toy trains and candles and goodness knows what!

And at last she was so tired of being in bed that she thought she would be naughty again and get up! So she slipped out of bed. It was cold, but Betsy-May didn't bother to put her slippers or dressing-gown on. She just wanted to run round before anyone came to see what she was up to.

She peeped out of the door. There was a light in the day-nursery. Bother! Nanny must be there, sewing. Where could Betsy-May go? The wind blew down the passage and she shivered.

"I'll creep up the little old attic stairs," thought Betsy-May.

"I'll go up to the attic, the little room under the roof where Mummy keeps her boxes and things, and see if I can find that old doll I once left there."

So up the attic stairs went the naughty little girl. She opened the attic door softly. Dear me, what a wind there was there! The window was open, and Betsy-May thought she would shut it. As she crept across the floor the door blew shut. Bang! What a noise it made! Betsy-May was sure Nanny would hear it, and she stayed quite still to see if she came. But she didn't.

"I'll shut the window," said Betsy-May to herself. "Then I'll look for my old doll, and take her down to bed with me. She must be so cold and lonely up here."

She shut the window, and then hunted round for the doll. She soon found it, thrown into a corner. Betsy-May shook the dust off Lucy, the funny old doll, and hugged her. "I'll take you down to my nice warm bed," she said.

She trotted across to the door and pulled at it. But dear me, the door wouldn't open! Betsy-May pulled and pulled. But when the wind had blown it shut, a catch had dropped down the other side of the door, and no matter what Betsy-May did, she couldn't open it! She was a prisoner in the attic!

Betsy-May didn't know what to do. If she called Nanny or Mummy, they would know she had been out of bed again, and they would be very cross indeed. But she couldn't stay in the attic all night. It was so cold.

Betsy-May shivered and pulled an old rug from a trunk. She wrapped it round herself, and then sat down on a pile of old garden cushions. She cuddled Lucy, and wished it wasn't so dark.

She felt so tired that she lay right down on the cushions with the old rug over her – and do you know, in about two minutes Betsy-May was fast asleep!

Yes – fast asleep in the attic-room all by herself, except for

Lucy the doll. Nobody knew. Nobody guessed she was out of bed.

It wasn't until Nanny went into the night-nursery to see if Betsy-May was all right, at ten o'clock, that she knew she wasn't in bed. Then what a to-do there was! What a lot of shouting and calling and rushing about!

"Betsy-May's gone! Where is she? Has anyone seen Betsy-May?"

The puppy-dog rushed about too, wuffing loudly. Every one was puzzled and upset. "Betsy-May! Wherever can she be?"

Somebody went up the attic stairs. But the door was locked on the outside. "She can't be in there," said Mummy. "The door is locked."

"We'll just have a look," said poor Nanny, who was dreadfully unhappy to have lost Betsy-May. She unlatched the door and opened it. She looked inside, and held up her torch, for there was no light in the attic-room. And there she saw Betsy-May fast asleep on the old cushions, cuddling Lucy the doll!

"Oh, there she is, there she is!" cried Nanny, almost crying for gladness. "She's asleep – and she must be so cold up in this room. She must have come to fetch her doll. I'll carry her downstairs."

So Betsy-May was carried downstairs, still fast asleep, and put into her bed with a hot-water bottle to make her warm. Mummy and Nanny and Daddy were so glad to have found her, but so worried because Betsy-May wouldn't stay in bed at night.

The first thing that Betsy-May thought of when she awoke the next morning was Peter's birthday party. It was to-day, to-day, to-day! She sat up in bed – and then she saw Lucy, the old doll, and remembered how she had gone to fetch her.

"And I don't remember coming back to bed again," thought Betsy-May, puzzled. "Somebody must have carried me back. Oh dear – now I shall get dreadfully scolded, I know I shall."

But nobody scolded her, though every one looked rather sad, because Betsy-May had been disobedient at night again. And then, as she was getting up, she sneezed. She sneezed and she sneezed – and then she coughed.

"Betsy-May! You've got a bad cold!" cried Nanny. "Look how your poor nose is running! Oh, what a cough too! Get back into bed at once."

"A-tish-oo!" said Betsy-May. "But it's Peter's party, Nanny. A-tish-oo!"

"Well, you can't possibly go to parties with a bad cold," said Nanny, bundling her back into bed at once. "You know that perfectly well, Betsy-May. Peter's mother would send you home if you went."

"But how did I get it?" wailed Betsy-May. "I didn't have a cold yesterday!"

"Betsy-May, you got it because you slipped out of bed again last night," said Nanny. "And you ran about in the cold without slippers or dressing-gown – and you spent half the night in the cold attic. So no wonder you have got a cold. You made us all upset and unhappy – and now you have made yourself ill and unhappy too. It is a great pity. But if

101

you want to make a fuss about it and blame anyone, you must scold yourself hard for being so silly."

So Betsy-May had to stay in and miss Peter's lovely party. She was very sad. But she didn't make a fuss and she didn't cry. She knew it was all her own silly fault.

And that night when Nanny kissed her good night, Betsy-May said: "You needn't sit in the day-nursery to-night, Nanny, in case I get out of bed. I shall never do that again. You didn't scold me at all about last night, but I've scolded myself well, and I've promised myself never to do such a silly thing again."

"And do you keep your promises to yourself?" asked Nanny.

"Always," said Betsy-May. And she does, you know, so you may be sure she will never be silly at night any more!

BETSY-MAY HAS A SURPRISE

Betsy-May wanted to go to school, but Mummy said no, not yet.

"Nanny can teach you your letters and how to count," she said. "You go to dancing every week, and that is quite enough just at present."

"It isn't really enough," said Betsy-May. "You see, Mummy, I do so want somebody to play with. And there are lots of children at school. I see them going along the road every day."

"Well, you have Tubby to play with," said Mummy. "He plays all sorts of games with you. You can't be lonely."

"Yes, I *am* lonely," said Betsy-May. "I'm very, very lonely. I want six brothers and sisters. Could I have them for Christmas?"

Mummy laughed. "I haven't enough money to buy you such a large family," she said. "Nanny, if Betsy-May is lonely, she must have more children to play with."

"Well, Peter goes to school now," said Nanny, "and Eileen is too big, and little Jane is rather a rude child. There are only the babies left – and they are too little for Betsy-May."

"Oh no, they're not!" cried Betsy-May. "I love babies! Let me play with them, Nanny. Ask them to tea, and you'll see how well I play with them!"

But Betsy-May found that the babies were most disappointing. Susan's little brother came to tea, and he was asleep all the time!

"How can I play with somebody who is asleep?" said

Betsy-May, after she had been shushed about twelve times for making a noise. "I like Bobby – he looks sweet and he smells like a rose. But I like him awake, not asleep."

The next baby that came was Rosemary, a small baby girl with bright golden curls. She smiled at Betsy-May.

"I want to hold her," said Betsy-May. So Nanny put her gently on Betsy-May's knee – but, oh dear, Rosemary screamed and screamed! Nanny had to take her away again. Then Rosemary stopped screaming at once and smiled.

"Doesn't she like me?" asked Betsy-May sadly.

"Oh yes, she likes you," said Nanny. "But she isn't used to you, you see."

"I should like to play with a baby who is *used* to me," said Betsy-May. "An awake baby, who likes being on my knee."

Then another baby came – a bigger one, called Ronnie. He sat on the floor and banged a rusk hard on the carpet. Betsy-May sat beside him. She showed him a little doll out of her dolls' house. The doll had hurt its arm, and Betsy-May had bandaged it neatly.

"Look, Ronnie," said Betsy-May. "Poor dolly! She has hurt herself."

Ronnie held out his hand and took the doll. He dug his finger into the doll's face.

"Don't squeeze her too tightly," said Betsy-May. "She has hurt her arm."

Ronnie took no notice. He went on poking at the doll's tiny eyes with his finger.

"Now give dolly to me, Ronnie," said Betsy-May. But Ronnie wouldn't! He held on to the doll and wouldn't undo his fingers at all. Betsy-May felt cross with him.

"Ronnie! You are hurting dolly. Give her to me," she said.

Ronnie put the doll's head into his mouth and stared at Betsy-May with his big blue eyes. Betsy-May gave a scream.

104

"Nanny! Come quickly! Ronnie's eating my doll! Oh, quick!"

Ronnie's Nanny gently took the doll out of Ronnie's mouth. She gave him the rusk that had fallen on his dress, and when he dropped the doll, she gave it to Betsy-May.

"He wasn't really eating it," she said. "Look, dry her head with your hanky."

Betsy-May went to her own Nanny. "Ronnie isn't very nice," she said. "He tried to eat my doll."

"Well, he didn't know any better," said Nanny. "If he was your own baby brother, I am sure you wouldn't mind."

"Oh, Nanny! Wouldn't it be lovely if I had a proper baby of my own!" cried Betsy-May. "I could see you bath him then – and I'd see him awake too, because he wouldn't always be asleep – and I could help you to push the pram – and he would have his own toys, so he wouldn't eat mine! Oh, Nanny, couldn't we buy a baby to keep for ourselves? I wouldn't be lonely then, would I? I could always go and talk to the baby, or look at him, if I felt lonely."

"Well, we'll see," said Nanny.

"That means we won't have one, I'm sure," said Betsy-May, who knew that when Nanny said "We'll see", it usually meant that what she wanted didn't happen.

But strange things began to happen, all the same. Once, when Betsy-May peeped into the spare-room, she saw a most beautiful cot, with blue muslin curtains and frills, standing all by itself in the middle of the floor. It was most extraordinary.

And another time, when she pulled open a drawer in the nursery chest that usually had her knickers and bodices in, she found a neat pile of tiny woolly coats and socks, much too small for *her* to wear.

She spoke to Nanny about it. "I shouldn't be surprised if a baby came to this house," she said. "I've seen funny things, Nanny."

"Have you really?" asked Nanny. "Well, I wonder if you would be pleased to have one here, a real proper baby of our own – or whether you would want it to go away and belong to somebody else?"

"Oh, I would never want it to go away!" cried Betsy-May. "I would love it for my own."

"Yes, but it would make me very busy, feeding it, and bathing it, and putting it to sleep," said Nanny. "I might not have as much time to look after you as I have now, Betsy-May. That might make you cross or sad."

"It wouldn't, Nanny, really it wouldn't," said Betsy-May. "You'd love me just the same, wouldn't you?"

"Just exactly," said Nanny. "More, I expect, because you would be the big one, then, and could help me such a lot."

"Fancy! I would be the big one!" said Betsy-May, and she felt important all of a sudden.

Now one afternoon Nanny and Betsy-May went for a walk, and when they came back Nanny suddenly got most excited.

"Come and see something!" she said in a whisper. So Betsy-May went to the spare-room with Nanny, and there, in the pretty blue cot, lay a tiny baby, with a red face, hardly any hair at all, and two of the tiniest hands you ever saw. He was asleep, and he looked like a live doll.

"Oh! Our baby has really come!" said Betsy-May in great delight. "Isn't it sweet? I wish it was awake."

Just as she said that the baby opened its dark eyes and looked straight at Betsy-May.

"It's looking at me!" said Betsy-May, and she gently touched the tiny hands. "Nanny, it's even got nails, look – so tiny you can hardly see them."

"It's a baby brother," said Nanny. "Won't he be pleased to know that he has a kind, big sister like you, Betsy-May. He is very lucky."

"I am lucky too!" said Betsy-May. "Where's Mummy? Let's tell her."

"She's lying down," said Nanny. "She has got another nurse for the baby for a few weeks, Betsy-May, till the little thing gets used to us all – and then Mummy says *we* may have the baby for our own, in our nursery! So we must be very busy turning out the cupboards and the drawers, getting ready for our little brother."

"It's not going to live in the spare-room then!" said Betsy-May. "It will live with us! Oh, Nanny, I'm so happy! I shan't be lonely any more. I shall always have our baby to look at and talk to. He can even eat my dolls if he likes!"

The month seemed such a long time – but at last it came to an end, and the day came when the baby was to go to live in the nursery. Betsy-May was so excited that she could hardly eat her breakfast. "I shall bath the baby at ten o'clock," said Nanny, "in the nursery by the fire. You must help me, Betsy-May. I shall want the rubber bath put up, and you must get me the sponge and the flannel and the soap ready."

"Oh, I will. I will!" said Betsy-May. So she did. And how happy she felt when she saw the baby kicking in its warm bath in her nursery!

"I'm lucky!" she said. "I've got somebody to share things with now – and it's nice to share, isn't it Nanny? Oh, here's Mummy! Mummy, the baby is ours now, and he's to live i the nursery! I shall love him best of all my toys!"

And now Betsy-May is no longer lonely. She doesn't want to go to school. She doesn't want other babies to play with. She has her own little brother.

He loves Mummy and he loves Nanny – but most of all he loves Betsy-May. He smiles and chuckles whenever she comes near, and Nanny often says: "Where's Betsy-May? Baby's crying, Betsy-May – he'll stop for you, but for no-body else. Come and talk to him, there's a dear!"

And doesn't Betsy-May feel proud and pleased then! You should just see her face!